Only Human

Only Human

Susie Boyt

review

For Kate Mackenzie Davey

One

The Braintrees were at each other's throats again. It was Friday afternoon and they were frightened of weekends. The ill-feeling that existed between this couple was not today as vivid as it sometimes was, but just now even that seemed like a sad thing, an additional loss.

Helen Braintree glared at her shoes, which were of chestnut suede with slender, well worn, two-inch heels. Her husband, in his highly controlled way, had just reeled off, quite calmly, a list of all the reasons she disappointed him. His long narrow limbs were loose and he arranged them gracefully round his person, like allies.

Between these two sat a low table on which paper tissues and a potted geranium and a ribbed plastic bottle of water were arranged.

'If I am so completely awful, what are we doing here?'

'Yes,' her husband answered her. Then, after a small pause, he offered, 'Am I right in thinking, then, that what you are saying is that you want things to come to an end?'

Roughly, Helen folded her hair away from her eyes,

tucking it into the neckline of her dress. 'Things?' she echoed dully.

'You must see we're wasting our time.'

'Are you saying our marriage is a waste of time or that coming here is?' Helen asked.

'Which are you saying?'

Next to the low table was Marjorie Hemming's chair. A woman in her very early forties, dark-haired and with exceptionally creamy skin, Marjorie was built on a generous scale – excessively curvaceous – her body a keen accumulation of flesh, with very little in the way of bone. The delights withheld and contained beneath the very proper racing-green tweed suit she wore had been variously hailed as angelic, angora-like, magnificent, marble and marshmallowesque. Only her legs, which she herself termed 'good', had kept on the straight and narrow. She was grateful to them, for they cut the richness of her upper portion. On a good day Marjorie viewed her body as a not-inconsiderable professional tool. For was not the obvious sensuality of her form, even as it just operated quietly and singly in the corner of the consulting room, an abstract reminder of the existence, of the importance, of pleasure?

The Braintrees came to see Marjorie, 'Mrs Hemming', every Friday afternoon for marriage-guidance counselling. This was their seventeenth session. They had been married no more than a year. Marjorie's interpretation of events was this: since he loathed himself in virtually every respect, Mark could not forgive Helen for liking him. Helen, meanwhile, felt his love her due. The more she tried to reach him, and this she did occasionally, the more Mark tried to escape her grasp. He saw the solution to their marriage as her leaving, but would not initiate a split himself, except by encouraging one on her side. She would not leave, partly because she said she loved him and partly because she did not want to 'give him the satisfaction'. And yet whenever she did withdraw slightly there was a substantial thaw on her husband's side and their life together briefly took off in the most delightful ways. And so they rolled on.

'Sometimes I wonder,' Helen ventured, 'whether we might have more success if we moved abroad, maybe, or to the country.' A graceful, pale smile appeared on her face as she spoke and, for a moment, she seemed less careworn.

'Are you out of your mind?'

'You suggest something, then?'

'I just wonder if we're beyond that.'

There was grave silence until Marjorie intervened: 'Do you think, at this point, it might be useful to think what it is that makes you both still come here?'

'You see,' Helen spoke up, 'what people like you forget is that, Mark and I, we still have so much in common.'

Mark looked intrigued. 'We do?'

'Yes. Perhaps we might spare a minute or two to see what it is you two really agree about.'

'Let's think.' Helen laughed anxiously. 'We both have a horror of children. Babies in particular. All the blood and shit and vomit!' Helen giggled, wriggling her hands as though those substances were lurking, with intent, in the air above.

'Well, quite.'

A minute passed slowly. It was understood by all that it was Mark Braintree's turn to make some sort of offering. Eventually he said, with a little humorous sigh, 'We neither of us suffer fools, do we, Helen?'

'Well, I know *I* don't. I've tried. I just can't do it.'

Mark raised an eyebrow provocatively and made a sound that began as a cough and ended an amused snort. It was meant to register approval. He moistened his lips and looked on the verge of speaking, but instead he merely made a curt bow with his head in his wife's direction.

'Well, it's true!' Helen protested.

'I don't doubt it.' Mark smiled. 'I've no doubts on that score at all,' he added, smoothing a small patch of skin on the edge of his cheek where there was a chickenpox scar.

'Well, good!' Helen bit her lip. Her cheeks were reddening and her pupils darted about jauntily in their moist sockets. A strong smile opened on her mouth to mirror her husband's. The Braintrees excelled at this kind of low-level strangulated flirtation. They could keep it up for hours.

Marjorie looked on with interest and some affection. She was fond of the Braintrees. She had clawed back couples in the past from far bleaker brinks. This had even got her into trouble once or twice. 'It's not for us to provide the cement for unworkable relationships, Marjorie,' cautioned Richard Adler, the director of the Wellbeck Centre where she worked, once casually with smiles and apologetic nods, and once more formally when a brief note had been scribbled to her on one of the Centre's pistachio-green correspondence cards. Marjorie had shrugged all this off, of course. Besides, she liked cement – its dark, powdery ooze, its scent. And you had to remember, all marriages were bizarre places, rife with signs and codes and unimaginable sharp practice where the more insane aspects of

4

human nature flourished, were endured, tolerated, overlooked, sought out and sometimes even admired. You did not need to be a genius to see that people were more unhinged in their behaviour with the very person to whom they were closest. It was the most natural thing in the world. Of course, the little untouchable regions that existed on the outskirts of a marriage or on its underside were always going to cast their shadows. No one was immune to strain and hollow feelings. But when they worked or even half worked! From her own brief, rosy-hued experience Marjorie knew, beyond doubt – there was nothing like it.

Marjorie Hemming was an emotional person. She craved concord and harmony the way other people need cigarettes or alcohol. She was not a saint. If she made a generous move, when driving, say, she did not like it to go unrecognised. She waited for the motorist's wave of acknowledgement, the pedestrian's grateful nod. And yet she did not hate conflict. She respected it. She saw it as a challenge. You could make so much out of it. It was grievous, fuming silence and blank neglect that characterised the worst situations. A meticulously detailed disaster was always more promising than an approximated one. She did not know why this was so, but she was sure. Marriage was an agreement to be entered into by grown-ups but when the participants were immature, that was when the problems came. Say you wanted to transform your wife into the ideal mother you had longed for as a child, hoping blindly that present-day attempts at change might spill some retrospective sweetness on to the past, or maybe you loved and loathed your workaholic husband for reinforcing your outrage at your own father's absence, because it was familiar, because it was horrible in exactly the same way . . . well, that's when you got into hot water. And yet everybody did these things. Everyone was afraid of truth and love. It was perfectly ordinary.

These sharp promptings from childhood had a monumental pull. And wasn't it true that the sensations of early youth were stronger and more affecting than any subsequent feelings? Marriage, other achievements, a ragged divorce – these sizeable events were really less intensely emotional than the day-to-day negotiations of a child's world. Was there a position Marjorie should have taken that would have rendered her more appealing in her mother's eyes? Marjorie did not know.

Marjorie Hemming truly considered herself to be grown-up – well, at work she did, buttoned tightly into tweed or velvet or felted wool, kempt hair, a floaty scarf at the neck to soften the overall effect. At home, however, mooning about in her husband's laceless walking-boots and a rose-festooned breakfast kimono – its bell sleeves itchy with a wealth of buttery crumbs – and mourning intensely the recent loss of her adored daughter to a student flat-share nine streets away, she was not so certain. She was a careful person – not exclusively so, of course: on the night of her husband's funeral seventeen years ago, her baby daughter had been sick and the sick had had a tiny metal bolt in it. But those were exceptional circumstances, she had not been herself. It was important to remember that. Also, her age was tricky. At forty-two was she an old-young person – at the last reaches of something raw and sharp – or was she really now a very, very young-old person who needed to greet and somehow shape the dim expanse of woolly time stretched out before her? It was true there were traces of grey in her hair, disguised, of course, but that was hardly a crime. Matters concerning her shape occupied her similarly. For instance, was she dumpy, always preferring a slab to a sliver, or was she, just quietly, just to the trained eye of the right kind of connoisseur, with her pert face and exceptionally luxuriant double-cream all-over body glow, something of a goddess? Recently she had noticed people staring at her with a new kind of intensity. What was the source of this sudden surge of interest? Had she effected some imperceptible change that caused people to peer?

Marjorie Hemming considered herself not a stupid person, but occasionally it dawned on her that her private thoughts, when scrutinised, would probably suggest she was less intelligent than she felt.

Marjorie blinked. Helen's voice was clear and her chin jutted sharply into the air.

'I'm so tired of everything. If he starts, I just won't be responsible for my actions.'

'Well – that will make a change!'

'When you say "starts", can you let Mark know what it is you don't want him to do? Be really specific,' Marjorie encouraged her.

'Just all that petty undermining stuff. I don't want to have to fend off your nasty comments all weekend. I know it's mainly carelessness, but I don't think you realise just how much . . . how little . . . And sometimes I think, pretty soon, there's only so much wear and tear a person can take . . . It stays with me, you know, like when you saw me across the room at Jane's party in my red-and-brown dress and came over and said I looked like a rat's abortion.'

'Did I say that?'

'Yes, you did.'

Mark paused to consider this comment. 'It's such a non-visual image, isn't it? I wonder what I was thinking. I can't believe you would take something like that seriously. You know my sense of humour!'

'Helen, can you say exactly to Mark what you *do* want him to do this weekend?'

'I want you to be nice. Don't want you getting at me all the time. Quarrelling. Picking fights. Half the time I think it's boredom as much as anything. He just seems to delight in driving me crazy. All that provocation – it's so tiring. And what you don't realise is with me a little would go such a long way. Practically *nothing* would make a huge difference, you know.'

'Well, I can't promise anything. I'm the person I am. I'm the same as when you married me. I haven't changed.'

'What do you make of that, Helen?'

'I'm not sure. It's all so confusing. It was a bad time for me then. I didn't have my eyes open. And he has changed. He used to be really fond of me.'

'"Used to be really fond of me". Have you any idea how pathetic you sound? For what it's worth, and I'm certainly not suggesting it's worth much, my feelings haven't changed. In fact, I don't think I've changed my mind about anything in years. I thought that was one of the things that made you so angry.'

'So is what you're saying that you *are* still fond of me?'

'Helen. Please. You know I've never gone in for that kind of talk.'

'You see what he's like? There's no friendliness. No warmth.'

'OK. Now that you've both had a chance to say one or

two things, I'm going to suggest something. It may sound a bit odd, but I'd like the two of you to decide that on Saturday and Sunday nights between, say, seven and ten, you both make an effort to be as kind and friendly as possible. If any arguments or conflicts arise, one or other of you will say that it has to be put off until after ten. During those three hours I want both of you to focus on doing what will make the other most happy. I'm now going to ask each of you what that would be. You go first, Helen.'

'I'd like the house to be quiet and I'd like to be sitting in a chair with some music on, cello music, perhaps, and a drink and Mark sitting nearby, maybe reading, and something cooking, and every so often, only occasionally, he'll look up and tell me something funny that he's reading or ask my opinion, and then after a while we'll have dinner and we'll just talk nicely without him finding fault or mocking me or putting me down.'

'What do you say to that, Mark?'

Mark looked reasonable. 'Heard worse. I think I can try to tread on eggshells for a couple of hours.'

'I don't know why he has to call it "treading on eggshells". It's so insulting. Mark?' Helen urged.

'Sorry, I was thinking of something else.' His eyes were fixed on the square, uncurtained window above Marjorie's chair. 'Do you see the flag on that building over there? I think it's Czech.'

'Let's not get distracted here. Will you agree to what Helen suggests, Mark?'

'Yes. I suppose so. But what do I get in exchange? What does she have to do?'

'What would you like Helen to do?'

'How should I know?'

'What you get is that I stick around for another week.'

Mark cleared his throat. 'Happy day,' he murmured drily.

'You beast!' Helen took an affectionate mock-swipe at her husband's head.

'Hey! She's beating me up! Surely that must be against the rules.'

'There are no rules,' Helen interjected. 'Unfortunately.'

Just then Mark pulled himself up to his full height in his chair. 'Is it time, now?'

Marjorie glanced down at her watch. 'Yes, it is time.'

'OK, then,' Helen murmured, gathering herself together, looping her arms through the handles of her squashy straw basket.

'I look forward to hearing how you get on.'

''Bye, now,' Helen said cheerily.

'Thank God that's over. It's like having a tooth pulled,' Mark was muttering under his breath.

'Quite,' Marjorie did not mutter under hers.

With the Braintrees safely on the other side of the door Marjorie watered her geranium to within an inch of its life and wolfed a handful of miniature gingernuts. She sat thinking for a moment, trying to take some kind of measure of the scene she had witnessed. Am I anything more than their audience? she wondered. A lot of the time anyway. But they do need me. At any rate, they need someone interested. She made one or two notes on a blank sheet of paper. She looked down at her husband's thin, gold-nibbed pen as it formed the artistically shaped characters.

The Braintrees are stuck [*she wrote*], and I'm starting to think it suits them. They say things out loud, but it isn't really any sort of a conversation. Self-dramatising tone — some of which seems to be for effect. Possibly playing with fire, not sure. Two options. (1) They need to do some proper work, make some kind of commitment to changing things Or B) Must decide to accept themselves as they are.

Even as a child she had held a fascination for the whole business, before she even knew the words. Why do people have relationships? What are they meant to mean? Why does my mother ladle out my father these huge platefuls of steaming food every night (her eyes slitted angry and hard) and he just pretends he hasn't seen?

That night, propped up by six downy pillows in bed, Marjorie peeled a pink grapefruit, scoring the skin with her thumbnail, lifting it off, dividing the fruit into segments and removing, carefully, the thick pith and pips. She felt the gaps between her fingers fizz and prickle as the juice ran down and her lips burned crimson from the acid taste, but she kept on eating. It was part of her bedtime routine. Bath, read, grapefruit, teeth, a pot of Sleeptight tea and sleep. Marjorie had a sleep problem. At night, in her head, insults tended to fly. Marjorie hoarded slights and slanging matches the way some people counted sheep, from the mundane Pig, the Stupid or Selfish Cow, to the more specific 'Spiteful, Self-Seeking, Fat Nazi Bitch' that had been barked by a middle-aged American man named Joshua Harrington to his placid English wife. It

Susie Boyt

had silenced the room, all right, all of them sitting bug-eyed, the wife a picture of dignity, practising her yoga breathing, and Marjorie noiselessly tapping her fingers on the blue-green inverted pleat of her skirt. Insults were everywhere. Threats were. They lurked darkly, waiting, waiting. And, of course, the margins for sexual disappointment were always going to be huge.

And then came the attempts at rationale, when rationale had nothing to do with it at all. One young man, a lawyer with a strong jawline and pale eyes, used to utter sentences such as 'You see, what it comes down to is, I need more reasons to love her than she seems to be able to provide.' Yet his fiancée, an older, sunnier, clear-skinned, even-keeled woman, had somehow managed to shrug it off: 'I don't know how you can say such things when I'm so happy and proud of you.' You could never predict what was going to cause the worst offence. And the things people used for consolation: 'It feels so much better with him hating me than when I have to hate myself.'

And then, of course, intimacy lent itself so well to deception. For some, that knowledge was simply too much to bear. The closer you came to someone, the more frankness and trust going around, well, it made everything instantly more possible – love, elation, absolute faith . . . complete betrayal. You only had to think of poor old Othello. And yet there were no obstacles that could not be overcome if the desire was really there.

Marjorie's insomniac head was big on theatrics. Her night thoughts were crammed with larger-than-life characters, the more outlandish of the cast and extras who had played out their scenes before her, jabbing their fingers hysterically at Marjorie's face in her little lamplit consulting room, nine to five, down the years. The radiant Italian waitress with the roving eye who set a cat among the pigeons at the restaurant manager's birthday party; the jet-haired doctor, nervous and aloof, who lanced the wife's boil that time and now she can't get him out of her mind; the Scottish woman's throat throbbing in its necklace of red beads as she told how her husband's daughter doused her walk-in wardrobe with twelve-year-old whisky and then threw in a lighted match. The rangy ex-wife, crazy with grief, who broke into the house last spring and dragged all the sheets off the beds.

The marriage props: the rejected crimson Christmas lingerie, the long honeymoons spent loafing on gondolas while longing for home, or canoeing over rapids, or head to head with a lion's roar through the eye of a jeep. As if life weren't dangerous enough! And all along the iron strong-held convictions chimed: 'Why, we do it this way because we always have!'

People came to Marjorie when they thought they saw the end in sight and the sighting alarmed them, or when they were bored or angry or guilty or sorry or wrong and did not know how to make good. They came with bruised hopes. They came incredulous – all their plumpest expectations buffeted and broken. They came because they had everything they wanted, all the ingredients of happiness, but still they were restless, discontent, lacking their moorings. They came because the very things that had sparked their unions ('Marcus was so sophisticated and relaxed and self-sufficient') were driving them apart ('He's so distant and impenetrable. The things I have to do to catch his attention. Like you wouldn't believe!'). They came because they no longer had the faintest idea what it was that had first caused them to care. Occasionally they came when other aspects of their lives were in turmoil, for in times of crisis, she had often observed, you sure need to know whom to love. And Marjorie, for her part, sat and listened acutely and evenly to everything that was said. She listened so hard sometimes, she felt the veins on her forehead bluish and smarting. Her standards were high by anyone's reckoning. To enter completely into the sensibility of each marriage, to try to approach each couple with the highest degree of respect and sympathy and ordinary soundness of mind and patience – to create an environment, a three-way partnership of deep trust where nothing is unsayable, however dark, for surely reconciliation is cheap when it does not acknowledge the darkest of human hours – this was her starting point. For the troubled souls who braved the Wellbeck Centre for Marital Studies, this was, in fact, the least she would do.

Sleep was now out of the question. Her head was a circus of disappointments and spectacular reconciliations (these she considered her speciality). Sometimes, as the hours available for repose grew fewer and fewer, Marjorie would restart her bedtime routine, the tea, the fruit, the teeth – everything. This was something she had done occasionally with her daughter in her pink-and-yellow toddlerhood. At eleven o'clock at night, when still May showed no sign of drowsiness, she would give her her supper again, bath her again, feed May her gnawed little beaker of milk and put her back into her bed. The doctor said she never had heard of a child so disinclined to sleep in her life. 'It could be acute intelligence, sleep simply bores her . . . or . . . or it may just be wind.' She told Marjorie to leave May crying in her cot, shut the door and eventually she would drop off. 'In cases like this it's really you or them. I have seen women hospitalised due to sleep deprivation – surely that's not what you want.' Marjorie held her tongue, but the doctor's advice left her seething. Leave her to cry herself to sleep – you might as well say put the baby with stones in a bag in the river.

It will be all right. You can always catch up on sleep when she's older, she cheered herself, when her daughter was small. And now May was seventeen, newly installed in a terrible little flat, while in her deserted bedroom there lingered a stale, inevitable void and the vague smell of mouse nests and STILL MARJORIE COULD NOT SLEEP.

Marjorie was back in bed again now. On her third cup of Sleeptight, which was the manufacturer's recommended maximum. She tried to flick away the discordant scenes that cluttered her night thoughts. It was only one o'clock in the morning. She had an hour to wait: if she was still awake at two she allowed herself some valerian drops, and if still awake at two thirty half a lemon-yellow Temazepam; both remedies made her feel sluggish and sullen on waking, which she hated. If the half Temazepam did not work there was always the other half or half a Valium at three and possibly the other half later on, or there was old-school Mogadon – but that didn't make her sleep, exactly, it just felt as though a large, dark weight had been placed on your head and nothing you could do would shift it so you just had to lie there, bludgeoned by some synthetic version of rest that really would fool not a soul. And if the Mogadon did not work – well! You could get into the hard core, the major line sedatives. One strip of pills, in her possession since the death of her husband seventeen years ago, warned you not to drive for seventy-two hours. She ought to throw them out, she really ought. More than likely all the sting had gone out of them over time. But. But you had to weigh it all up. Sleeplessness could make you doubt everything, from your own powers to the sincerity of your loved ones. Hadn't people admitted dishonestly to heinous murders in order to get a few hours' rest? Hadn't they committed them? Recently Marjorie had been feeling so tired that she regularly pictured her body mass stretched and cratered with ragged oval holes and herself slipping down them in fast, circular motions, like water coursing down a plug.

Her head pounding with the heavy ache of exhaustion, Marjorie's thoughts grew darker and more anxious — a sort of insomniac's remorse. She made a tower of all her life's errors and blanched as it loomed over her, inexcusably tall. She had made so many mistakes and almost all were large ones. This was true of everyone, no doubt, but Marjorie's were worse. With her daughter. With work. (She had once counselled a couple for almost a year before she realised that the wife had been desperately trying to communicate in all sorts of unspoken ways that her husband was prone to bouts of violence.) She had not behaved well after Hugh died. At first she had made the requisite effort. Everyone said she was managing brilliantly. 'You're so strong, you're so brave,' they decreed. And it was true that the management had been award-winning. She was a grief expert. She gave tips to no one in particular. 'You know, you really can't mourn all day long,' she said. 'You need lots of time off. I find it works best if you take a couple of hours every other day to break down,' she said. 'That way it doesn't get out of control. And don't be afraid to dip into the biscuit barrel either! It's not a time to stint yourself.' Who was this numb, blithe lunatic, speaking knowingly, with jokes and recommendations, from the body of a twenty-six-year-old? She had got amphetamines from the doctor so that May might have a reasonable Christmas, and she had certainly gone to town, decorating even the cereal packets with robins and tinsel and glittery stars for the small baby, but after Christmas – well, she had not been good. Hugh's presents sat unopened under the Christmas tree until March, when she burned the skeletal orange branches in a bonfire. What to do with a dead person's presents? Was it wrong to stuff them under the bed? (For all she knew they were still there.) Through tiredness and misery she had done some unspeakable things, and still the compliments rolled in. 'You're such a coper!' her sister had said, on the telephone from Canada. They were not on good terms. Belinda was not the kind of person who would have a husband die on her. She wouldn't have stood for it. In grief you were a coward and a liar and a cruel manipulator of people and, worse than that, you – Ssssh, she said to herself. Sssssh. Marjorie attempted to quieten her mind. When trying to get to sleep you had to make yourself as boring and low key as possible – it was the same when you were trying to get a child off. She would have given her eyes to have May asleep on the top floor right now.

'Come on, then.' She rallied herself, semi-stern, business-like, a little anxious about the tightening sensation on the left side of her chest. 'Come on, now,' she said again, coaxingly this time, her tone kindly, a little parental. Marjorie hummed under her breath and brought to mind her husband's mild profile, his inclined head, the slightly concerned smile that was the habitual expression of his mouth in repose. He had been a great blessing and she counted him. She turned herself over in the sheets. She had never in her entire life got to sleep lying on her right side, but it was worth a try. The cotton was cool and silky on her limbs. She prodded her stomach disapprovingly with her thumb. The room was silent and the curtains, which spilled in a street-lamp's glare, were fashioned from ancient green-and-white striped silk.

She was thinking quietly now, patting the clammy flesh on her legs and staring at the ceiling. Counting your blessings was an art that was dead. People looked interested when you referred to it and asked you to explain, as if it were a complicated dish on a menu in French, or some highly technical term. And yet it was easy to fall at the first fence. If you listed your blessings not as they came to mind (in order of appearance) or in historical order, but instead in order of importance, then you would always come unstuck. If you concerned yourself with the status of each particular blessing it really went against the spirit of the thing. You could spark off all sorts of anxiety attacks over whether you loved the children more than your husband (if you were lucky enough to have both). And then when you had truly resolved which should come first, there was always a surplus of guilt and regret for the other side.

Eventually Marjorie felt something softening in her mind, some genuine kind of closing off and giving in, and the first pale waves of sleep began to steal over her exhausted frame.

Suddenly, from below, there came a loud crash followed by cursing. Frank, the man who rented the basement flat, was throwing things again. A nervy and ashen-faced Latin teacher by day, who was usually reeling from the spite and bile of the boys he taught, by night he painted dark portraits mainly from his imagination.

Sometimes, Marjorie mused, the world he lived in did not entirely suit his needs. He really lacked the temperament for young boys, there was no knockabout to him — and his after-hours painting sessions presented him with too much solitude. Even his hands, with their soft fluttery fingers, revealed him as delicate and highly strung. Yet his vulnerability was not of the sort that made you want to care for him, it was an eager, more discomfiting thing. It was embarrassing. Four years ago he had had an exhibition that Marjorie had visited in a small tea-shop adjacent to the Thames. To be neighbourly she had bought a round canvas — a portrait of a woman with flowers, all done in greens — and it hung in her bedroom over the little iron fireplace, looking out at her dully when she could not get to sleep. But this had proved a disastrous move: Frank, overwhelmed with gratitude, had interpreted her purchase as a romantic overture. He had written her a comprehensive love letter praising her milkmaid complexion, her hair, her limbs, her movements which he compared to swans, her manner which at once thrilled and soothed, her intelligence which recalled the most ardent librarians of his student youth. Even her gums came in for admiration — he called them 'plum-tender!' But when she had ducked and shied from every meeting he suggested (a cosy hiking trip in Wales, an excursion to a ruined cottage, which, when he read of it in a travel supplement, exactly matched one that featured in a recurring nightmare of his), their friendship eventually returned to one of eager hellos and thank-yous and let-mes and other brief and awkward shows of doorstep politeness. Marjorie did not hold it against him. In fact, she welcomed the awkwardness. In a strange sort of way it was a comfort. It felt familiar. It was living.

Occasionally a model came to sit for Frank, a big woman with a Slavic flavour to her appearance. Marjorie had once caught sight of this creature preening herself in the basement area, applying powder from a brass compact and, in broad daylight, swiftly drawing off a pair of thick tights in advance of her assignation. As she tugged deftly at the black nylon mesh she took quick bites of a hamburger, which dripped grease and red-and-yellow sauce on to the flagstones below. It was quite a feat she performed, this fast-food escapology. Marjorie was glad his model was tough because when the portraits were not going well Frank tended to swear and smash things. For waking her from what was probably her only real stab at sleep, Marjorie could have strangled him. She thought of going downstairs to make her complaint in person, there and then, rattling at the interconnecting door until he came to her in his paint-sodden navy overalls – he even got paint on his nose – and her in her dressing-gown, with thick night cream in greasy wedges on her face. 'What the hell are you playing at?' she would scream. 'What kind of time d'you call this?' One side-effect of doing the marriage counselling was that she could not have any sort of domestic spat without feeling like a plagiarist of the worst sort. She was so tired: in her exhaustion she might confuse things terribly. She could shout out anything that sounded vaguely strong and meaningful. 'I've given you everything and you're just throwing it back in my face!' Well, that would hardly do. She drew herself out of bed, ready to make her sortie, bracing her numb limbs for the journey down the four flights, fine-tuning her opening attack, tightening the splayed cord of her robe to avoid any spillage – but almost immediately she got back into bed and enfolded herself in the squashy bedclothes. 'Are you out of your mind?' she asked.

That was it now. Sleep was an impossibility. Even when she was married this dropping-off business had eluded her. Sometimes she had asked her husband to talk blandly with her in the evening, to help her unwind. He had perched on the edge of his chair, in his immaculate work clothes, the side light casting an amber shade in his chestnut-coloured hair. His slippers had little brass zips at the sides and his face was creased with humour and sympathy. Marjorie wore a forgotten apron of black gingham over olive green devoré, and on her suede evening shoes there was a fine dusting of cornflour.

'A lot of people think the weather's a tiny bit unseasonable,' Hugh would say, 'but d'you know what? I'm not really so sure,' his voice monotonous, his eyes and mouth comically expressionless and limp. Marjorie stifled a giggle.

'The problem with this country is that no one ever does anything any more, not like the old days.' He'd sigh briefly. 'Things really are not what they used to be. Did I forget to mention that tomorrow I may just buy some eggs?' he added. 'Something like that anyway.' Marjorie hung on his every word. 'Can't quite decide.'

'Did you have something in mind for them?' she'd ask.

'For what?'

'For the eggs.'

'Oh, don't know, really. Not too bothered. It's all much of a muchness. Poached, some prefer, or scrambled. Coddled. Fried is always popular. Boiled. I do find omelettes a strain. Half-way through them I sometimes feel I'm losing the will to live.'

Marjorie sat bolt upright in her low chair. 'That's not boring,' she said.

'I'm sorry,' he said. 'You know it doesn't come naturally.'

'Try harder!'

'All right. So sorry. Yes, eggs – well, it's a hotbed of controversy. Some people like fried eggs, and then other people really prefer the white to the yolk, but I think both can be good, but only if you're in the right mood. But, then, other people say the secret to eggs is the bread and butter, but I don't know if that's a little too rich for the average palate, if you see what I mean. Salt, of course, pepper – white pepper, if you're a gourmet. No preference myself. What's the difference really?'

Is that what boredom was, absence of feeling?

All feelings were good when they were honest and heartfelt and true, thought Marjorie, rustling the bedclothes. Dawn was breaking now. Through a chink in the curtains she could see bars of sunlight and a raw green tree and the first stirrings of a slack breeze. Sometimes it seemed that, really, there was scarcely any difference between good and bad. She hoped with all her heart that this was true. Bad people were not worse than good people, of that she was sure, only more miserable, possibly, and usually less adept. Their thoughts, feelings and actions certainly had an equal validity. She shuffled her body down into the bed and absently traced the edge of her face with her hand. Or was it just that goodness and badness mingled together were a far better proposition than goodness alone, because goodness alone equalled a sort of bleached insanity and bad in isolation was so rare as to be almost non-existent, give or take the obvious exceptions?

Of course, not everyone could run to feelings. When your husband dies without warning and his body is scarred out of recognition and only his steel watch-face really identifies him – the one you had engraved for a wedding present – as well as the odd scrap of clotted hair and the faded blue of his shirt fabric, barely blue at all now, and everywhere white tubes and pumps and screens and drips, all in the frozen black middle of the night, what sort of defence are feelings? They had no place when there was a small baby on your hands at all hours of the day, in your arms, sleeping on your chest at night, sucking hard at your nipples until they were crimson and raw, and spots of blood streaked the milk?

Her daughter was seventeen now and Marjorie's admiration vast.

'Mum, why do you always laugh when I come into the room?' May slouched into the kitchen with a half-smile in the dark, baggy boys' clothing favoured by all her friends, her unwashed face, oily dark-blonde fringe and the golden sleepy dust crusting her eyelashes trying and failing to mask her natural beauty. She fiddled with her hair idly, splitting a frayed end right down to the root. She looked like a starlet on her day off, Marjorie thought. The cheekbones, the milk-and-roses skin and the lime-coloured eyes . . . and the cigarettes and the nibbled fingernails. 'Just happy to see you, that's all.'

'Oh, Mum! Get a grip, yeah?'

You couldn't let your children see how much they were loved. It would kill them.

Two

In the heart of London there are still many nameless
pockets of life and love and industry that lie anonymously in the
spaces between better recognised territory. These stray regions
located half a mile behind a mainline railway station, say, or
in the abandoned triangular plots between three landmarks
unwilling to share their names (taxi drivers require several
reference points to place them) are often quieter than the
spaces they border, and stranger and less certain of their
weaknesses and strengths. Many of the properties in such
streets look makeshift or ill-conceived or like the backs of
houses. Often little thought has been given to symmetry or
overall design. But their residents harbour pride and shame
in equal part at their forgotten situation, for a mere shift of
the light can transform these forlorn places into brilliant happy
secrets in a second.

Homer Rise was such a messy little back-street, crammed
with mews houses, double-width garages, a modern development of studios, one or two surprisingly tall Georgian
properties with slate-tiled upper storeys, a large, brightly lit

---

osteopathy clinic and a gloomy, low-built, fume-caked mansion block. Marjorie's house was exceptionally narrow, but its flat front and little low-key 1820s flourishes lent it a dignified air. Grey-painted brick with five pairs of front windows and a black front door, it resembled a severe child's drawing of a house with its curtains looped symmetrically in quarter-circles at each window and its shiny railings and its stack of black chimney-pots swirling smoke. The slim little row with its heroic name had been home to Marjorie for nineteen years. The house had come with her husband. He had shown it to her the day they met, and she had never quite gone home after that. It was a boyish abode, its cracked white walls crammed with all manner of pictures, its dark floorboards covered with rugs and books piled everywhere and myriad curvaceous, nurseryish armchairs and dining chairs and desk chairs and slatted kitchen chairs that, all in all, seemed so prominent they were almost like fellow residents. On a high shelf in a side room Marjorie spied a stuffed owl that was intensely sinister. She darted into the owl room and, glancing at herself briefly in the angled mirrors of a walnut dressing-table, pinched some twists of colour into her cheeks. In the narrow wings of glass she looked so animated suddenly. She barely recognised herself, but she knew straight away it was good. Breathlessly, she followed Hugh to the top-floor bathroom and climbed the tiny flight of white wooden steps through the trap-door in the attic, which opened out directly under the moon. She clutched at the ribbed hem of her grey jersey with cool fingers, her stomach prickling against the wool and the wind. They stood in the night air, several paces apart, shaking with cold as they scoured the black sky for stars. But there were no stars, just still trees and the dull collage of city

roofs: red, grey and blue-black, stretching out beyond them
for miles.

All the space in Marjorie's house had a provisional quality,
as though each room was a passage or store leading to larger,
more open parts. There was the suggestion of imminent width
and perfume and leisure as you picked your way through the
different floors and the abundance of barely furnished small
rooms, some oak-panelled, that implied there was something
spectacular to come, a vast salon with a sprung floor overlook-
ing beautiful lawns, a galleried area with rare pictures at the
very least . . . something that made you know you were in for
a grand surprise. Well, you were not. Upstairs, the house was a
maze of narrow rooms whose windows trickled condensation,
resembling half-landings or box rooms or studies, and even on
that first visit there were three or four chambers dressed with
no more than a pair of chairs, a dusty fireplace, a gaunt table
or a lamp and a corner basin. It was really a skinnier, more
austere building than you would ever know from its outside.
But the house was not to blame for its limitations. It was just
a case of mistaken identity.

After Hugh died everyone seemed to assume she would
knock through, but the thought appalled her. If her home
was little more than a stack of vacant bed-sits that did not
know how to tap into their potential, Marjorie did not care.
And the downstairs was practical, a sky blue reception area
leading directly from the front door, with two louche-looking
armchairs and a squashy sofa upholstered in pale ticking and
a television and a scrubbed wooden table, linked by a small
corridor to a square of black-and-white tiled kitchen with
high wooden shelves to all sides, and a serving-hatch easing

communications between the two, and beyond the kitchen a tiny pantry, with a drop-leaf grey Formica table, and beyond that a minuscule utility room with a Belfast sink in one corner and a twin-tub and a wired glass sliding door that shielded a lavatory with a dark-green-painted wooden seat. Marjorie had no complaints. She liked the separate parts, the connecting passageways and box rooms, which were, in fact, destinations in themselves. What it lacks in width, she pronounced, it makes up for in height. In any case, deep down, as the years went on, she often felt that the bachelorish, segregated setting provided a good foil to her own carefully arranged femininity.

Homer Rise connected several important thoroughfares like a ladder. Beyond its narrow western tip you could spy Arab men seated at night outside cafés, smoking bitter-smelling pipes and spearing blackened lamb cubes or sipping mint tea under the red neon glare of a huge cinema complex. To the east, the streets were clogged and choking with cars making courageous escape bids from London, and if you went north a little bit there was a prosperous high street where people ordered French birthday cakes or hand-smocked children's party wear or something highly scented for the bath.

But Homer Rise itself was an almost silent street, with an abandoned air. All around life was being lived, but it was not quite being lived on Homer Rise. And yet the life that there was in the immediate vicinity was all so particular. For instance, the red-brick hospital in the parallel street was Eye Casualty Only. Children with black patches or wads of white dressing taped to their faces were not an uncommon sight. In a bordering lane the Little Shoe Company catered solely for adults with extremely small feet, boasting miniature red patent stiletto court shoes and tiny wedge-heeled denim pumps that looked almost as kinky in a size one or two as they would have in a man's fourteen. This was overlooked by an outlet that supplied lamps specifically to the hotel trade, and Nuts about Nuts, an emporium selling nothing but sweet and salty organic kernels from around the globe. The owner was nuts' foremost champion, apportioning to them life-lengthening qualities as well as the more commonplace nutritional benefits. To some of his produce he had given pet names. (Marjorie once heard him address a vat of Israeli pinenuts as My Little Pirandellos.) One highly specialised boutique followed another. Recently a shop selling wholesale salon units to the beauty-parlour trade had sprung up, and in the window there were rows and rows of manicurists' tables upholstered in buttoned white vinyl with chrome shelving and a little swing-out stall for the beauty therapist to sit on, incorporated into the design. Next door, half obscured by scaffolding due to a thorough refurbishment programme, there was a chess and bridge superstore. Opposite was a wig shop, a colourful Swedish grocer's, and a place that sold elaborate confectionery sculptures, life-sized mermaids fashioned from white chocolate for your wedding party, say, and this gave on to a tiny Arabic ladies' hairdressing salon with a closed room for Hajeb. Seven streets away – a twelve-minute walk or four shaming stops on a single-decker bus – was the Centre where Marjorie worked.

Of course, there were fruiterers and a Chinese ironmonger's whose wares spilled out on to the pavement, and an acrid-smelling dry-cleaner's that packed up shirts in pink candy-striped bags, and a newsagent's and the Gammon Rasher café and a dusty builders' merchant, which boasted seventeen sizes of hammer arranged in descending sizes in a glass-fronted display panel opposite the double doors, but Marjorie hardly noticed these, except when evening fell and she made shame-faced dashes to one of the all-night shops, hovering over the children's selection packs or the violet-coloured Swiss family-sized bars often for almost half an hour before choosing one or two, and even then telling the assistants, many of whom did not speak English, 'It's not for me. Oh, no!' Occasionally, when her resolve was high, she would exit these mini-marts with just a few cans of a low-calorie pineapple and grapefruit crush she quite liked, then slowly make her way home, undefended and with a hollow in her heart.

Marjorie's telephone was ringing as she walked through the front door, valiantly dragging behind her the eight carrier-bags that comprised her weekly shop. At the supermarket something odd had taken place by the checkout. An elderly woman in a sharply belted hound's-tooth trouser suit had come up to her as she was arranging her shopping on the conveyor-belt. She stared hard into Marjorie's face, then bent to inspect her selection of groceries, sniffing disapprovingly. 'No better than the rest of us,' she had mumbled, looking aghast at the yellow rubber gloves, the own-brand leaf tea, the six-pack of fifteen-denier hose. Marjorie smiled. Why, she would be the first to admit it.

Marjorie disentangled the numb crooks of her fingers from the plastic handles and dropped her coat on the rush mat by the front door where several other discarded garments lay. She was weary and felt herself a little askew. It was Audrey, the receptionist from the Wellbeck Centre, on the line. Marjorie pictured her frizzy grey hair pulled off her face by a rubber band, her head framed by the many jokey postcards that hung in her little cubicle by the entrance to the waiting room. 'I'm not mad I'm just on a sanity break' and 'My other brain's a genius.' Was it meant to be funny? Audrey's voice was hoarse and jumpy. 'Sorry to disturb. It's just the Braintrees rang, asking if they might have an emergency session with you. They say they can't wait until next Friday. I spoke to Mrs B. She said . . . well, her exact words were, I noted it down, "Some new information has come to light." It's all very irregular, they know, but they wonder if you could squeeze them in before their next sesh. Unquote. I said I didn't know if I could reach you but I'd pass on the message soon as. They said they could see you first thing Monday morning. They'd be more than grateful. I know your first appointment next Monday is at ten fifteen, so it's not unfeasible, but it just depends on . . . well—'

'Give me a minute to think, could you, for a second?'

'I know. Don't ask much, do they?'

Marjorie made some calculations. The Braintrees did not generally express urgency. They had never even acknowledged that their visits to her were anything other than a grim punishment for private, non-specified crimes, and here they were, actually calling for her help. It was a compliment, really. She would grab it by the horns. 'Would you tell them I'll make a space for them at ten past nine?'

Marjorie had a copy of the Braintrees' file in the third-floor landing cupboard (locked in accordance with the recommendations of the counselling body to which she was affiliated) and she mounted the three flights of stairs with gusto. Seconds later she was lying on her front on the air-blue bedroom carpet, propped up on her elbows, with a faded Paisley eiderdown, and the Braintrees' notes fanned out in front of her. (It was in this attitude that Marjorie had done her homework as a teenager and then a student – 'An anxious and unhappy poet afraid of sex and death and God. Discuss'.) Straight away her head was brimming with suggestions as to what had caused the Braintrees to make their uncharacteristic request. Request? It was practically an order. How did people have the confidence to be so demanding? Marjorie did not know. She examined, minutely, their case. Her first ever session with the Braintrees was outlined in some detail. It had been a strangely exhilarating meeting. 'Help! We can't seem to stop making each other miserable!' was Helen's opener, the blithe delivery underwritten by deeply smiling schoolgirlish eyes and her husband's hand on her knee. Marjorie remembered it so clearly: the sheer nervous energy that had entered the room with the couple had seemed almost exotic, the bright panic and the flashes of recognition that had sometimes followed, and now and then the unconscious putting out of a hand from one to the other, for rebuke often but at other times for steadiness or some kind of confirmation. Mark had cleared his throat eagerly. 'They say the first year of marriage is the worst but – my God!'

'For all their poised scrapping,' Marjorie's notes said, 'the pair seem happy and in love. Possibility: they are happier making each other miserable than either would be making self miserable singly. Possibility: if Bs weren't miserable would be really quite distraught!'

A frenzied pleasure stole over Marjorie's brain, stimulating and intense in the way that boiling hot tea with something sweet is, or the proximity of your baby's watery-powdery admiration,

32

or beautiful clothes in your size, or capacious, lovingly prepared meals. She rolled up the sleeves of her heather-coloured silk-knit jersey. This stuff is good! she thought. It was warm outside – autumn warm – and through the part-opened window a fledgling breeze lapped at the hem of the curtains. In almost every single session she had seen the Braintrees they had made a comment along the lines of 'We're really not that unhappy.' It was almost a catchphrase with them.

'Do they mean, "we're not unhappy enough"?' Marjorie had scrawled a note. 'Is being only quite unhappy a reason not to take action? Not to make changes? Not to put in the required, well, leg work, if you can call it that? Is it, of all bad states, for this reason, the very worst?'

She returned to the file cupboard to look up in a book a Milanese case study that had been published recently in a journal for which she had taken out a subscription. The Italians had some revolutionary ideas. One institute had pioneered a brand of intervention called the Paradox of which they were extremely proud. This involved asking a couple to do the opposite of what you thought would help them most in the hope that, of their own accord, they would rebel against your authority, say you were out of your mind and effect the very changes that you originally thought would improve the situation. Marjorie was unsure. Was it not disrespectful to treat adults as hapless children? Was it not an insult to children?

When she came back into the room there was chaos. Papers were everywhere (sixty pages) dancing round the edges of the skirting caught up by the wind, under the bed, and at that very moment one was in danger of floating out of the window. She

dived over to the far side of the room and grabbed it, banging
the window shut as she did so. She shuffled the papers together
and peered under the bed to rescue another twenty leaves of
script. The underbed area was carpeted with thick dust and
crammed with all manner of unneedable items: lone socks,
spineless paperbacks, bits of a broken alarm clock. Marjorie
sneezed and gathered up the script as best she could, pushing
up her sleeve so as not to dirty herself, reaching into the far
dark corners. Suddenly her fingers touched something woollen
and crackly. She caught at it with her left hand, but she had
underestimated its weight. It was heavy and long, like some
kind of bulky stuffed limb. A Guy Fawkes crammed with balled
newspaper, reprieved at the eleventh hour, she thought; some
long-forgotten *papier-mâché* tribute from May's early childhood.
She pulled again.

A thick grey-green man's over-the-knee sports stocking (of
the sort that suggested cold dawns spent fishing) emerged at
the end of her fingers, packed tightly with faded red-and-green
Christmas parcels. The wool was papery in her hands, the
packages sealed with tape that was crisp and yellow with age.
Blithe robins and snowmen peered out from the wrapping,
demented with mirth, almost insane. Had she put together this
childish Christmas offering for Hugh the winter he had died? It
was in her style. She remembered that in the long weeks before
May was born they had both given much thought to Christmas
shopping to distract themselves. And yet she had no memory
of its production. Her mind went blank as to its assembly or
design. Some of the gift wrap featured a red-and-white bloated
Santa slumping under the weight of his present sack, or was it
from the bulbous glass of beer in his hand? She dimly recalled

his appeal. Had she had a hand in his choosing? And now he looked on the verge of cardiac arrest.

When viewed from its most impressive angle, Marjorie's childhood was comprised of sixteen spectacular Christmases. Her mother's habitual love of what was bright and sharp attached itself wholeheartedly to the season. At Christmas her children had been less of a burden: they permitted the excess, the extravagance. They justified it. For the rest of the year she had been a person of high spirits but she had no warmth. There were her rages, which were frequent and violent and inspired in Marjorie awe and respect, after which there sometimes came a fair imitation of warmth, a glow like that of a plastic log with an electric orange ray, but for all who hung by her it was quite clear the heating element had gone.

Gingerly, Marjorie undid the first package. She chose one that already wore its wrapping in shreds. Through the paper she could feel soft fabric. Was it a tie, she wondered. Surely she could not have been so boring, and yet being boring had been an elevated trait in her married household. It was something they had joked about. Boring people made good parents. Boring people got a good night's sleep.

The present was a stack of cotton lawn handkerchiefs from the 1950s embroidered with childish scenes from life. One depicted a woman in an apron, bending to remove a hot pie from a stove, with three little brown embroidered zigzags indicating steam hovering above the crust. One showed a couple in evening clothes holding cocktail glasses, their heads thrown back as they laughed at (was it?) witty drawing-room anecdotes. The next showed a portly man sitting behind a large desk with a cigar in one hand looking confident and wealthy. The material was limp and bitter-smelling, the embroidery a little too coarse for the weight of the fabric. Had she collected them for Hugh? It was the sort of thing he would have quite liked, was it, with its direct appeal to delicate feminine instincts? Was it? She had seen similar things in Bell Street market quite recently. Was it the sort of purchase you could forget? And then, suddenly, the handkerchiefs clawed at her heart. Their post-war optimism shot her married episode so far back into the past that Marjorie thought she was going to cry.

She decided to try the next package, which slipped easily out of its wrapping. It contained a tin of talcum powder printed with lilies-of-the-valley. She twisted round the brass lid until its bevelled holes lost their protective covering and shook a fine cloud of white powder on to the back of her hand. She raised it to her nose and sniffed. Nothing came. Then it hit her. These presents had not been meant for Hugh. They were his presents to her. She sat back on the floor and a strange kind of ache spread out in her throat. It tasted exactly the same as the feeling she'd had in her mouth when he had died. She pushed the stocking tidily back under the bed and wrapped her arms round herself. Rocking gently back and forth she crooned a self-lullaby. She tried to take solid breaths but the inhalations were thin and airless, or like the sour air from a long-closed room. After a while she went into the bathroom and gargled with red mouthwash.

That evening Marjorie met her schoolfriend Bette for a bite to eat, as she did almost every Saturday night. They had a standing order for each other at eight o'clock in an Italian restaurant, which was called La Scala, where once a month an opera singer warbled on a little wobbly podium in front of the kitchen doors between the hours of nine and twelve.

Bette had a new plum-coloured suit with cherry red paillettes on the collar and the shallow hem of the skirt. 'It's a bit much,' she confided, 'but it makes me feel like a country-and-western star.'

'I think it's just the right amount,' Marjorie said.

Bette worked in a bank, something to do with currency conversions. Her husband – her ex-husband – was baby-sitting the six-year-old twins. As she entered the restaurant, always exactly ten minutes late, and Marjorie rose to greet her from the table where she waited, reading something work-related such as *Learning from Divorce* or *The Guide to Good Enough Marriage*, Bette always said the same thing. With an exaggerated smile and a minstrel's shaking of her palms, she would yelp, 'Marjorie! Look! No kids!'

Marjorie wore a jade knit dress with elbow-length sleeves and a bone-coloured belted mac, which gave her the look, she felt, of a spry lady detective, intriguing, intrepid. If she also appeared well insulated – well, it was hardly a tragedy and, besides, the neckline of her dress was lowish and invisible under the coat's collar. With high patent shoes and sheer stockings lending her elegant foundations, only the harshest critic could think her uninteresting-looking. She chewed at a breadstick as if she had not a care in the world but it was so hard she thought her teeth would break. Absently she brushed sharp crumbs from her lap. 'That colour really suits you,' she said. 'You should wear it all the time.'

'I was about to say the same thing to you.'

'You don't think it's a bit tinned-peas?'

'Only in the best way.'

'Hugh liked me in green,' Marjorie murmured.

She closed her eyes briefly and thought, for a second, about the life they had shared in Homer Rise, every movement punctuated by Hugh's huge collection of hulking great chairs, but what really lingered were sensations of deep silence alternating with high festivity, which was how they had lived out their marriage. It was like a holiday from all her ideas about herself: the peaceful contentedness, the loose delights. Yet there was no doubt she had been that person with those belongings. She had no doubt she could have easily kept it up all their lives. She felt her husband's arm lying lightly across her breast and happiness travelling softly along her own limbs. She had not known she was able but somehow the early sadness had drained out of her. It was his doing, his being.

'I know,' Bette said soothingly, her eyes bent significantly. 'I know.'

At school Marjorie and Bette had formed a secret society of two, which met before lessons in a dank corner of the school library. Beside the peeling cream walls and the boiler's gruff, mechanic roar, they gathered chiefly to despair of certain of their classmates, who seemed to them shockingly immature. 'SHE DID WHAT?' 'ARE YOU SURE?' Marjorie and Bette shook their heads and rolled their eyes. There were girls in their form who actually hung around in the park behind school in the early evenings with the express purpose of meeting boys. Sometimes the boys brought cider and lemonade. Bette was thirteen, Marjorie twelve. Bette's parents were passionately interested in everything Bette said and thought and did. They bought her a pet hamster, which she named Julie Christine.

The school had no uniform but the society had its own pink-and-purple striped velour sweatshirt and a heart-shaped badge. It had rules of conduct involving loyalty, secrecy and honour. Bette's husband had left four years ago. Not even for someone else! Bette had complained at the time, her face electric with outrage, humour and shame in equal parts, the corner of her eyes betraying a propensity for mild hysteria. He felt, he had tried to explain, how to put it exactly?, that he was unsuited to married life. That it didn't agree with him. Thing was, you see, it made him feel trapped and anxious, and on balance he'd rather live alone at the other end of the street.

Just then huge steaming plates of spaghetti arrived, bathed in red sauce. Both women removed their outer garments and clinked their glasses of wine with gusto.

'How are the girls doing?'

Bette's girls were her pride and joy. From what Marjorie could surmise the three of them spent most of their spare time bundled on top of each other on the kitchen floor or on the sofa or on the hall carpet, repeating over and over again, 'I love you.'

'Nice work, if you can get it,' Bette said, all smiles. She paused and took a shallow breath. 'Have you seen much of May lately? Or I expect, what with everything . . .'

'Little bit. We're both so busy now it's term-time. You know what it's like.'

'Oh, absolutely. I know half the time there's never a minute for anything. Why do we all lead such busy lives?'

'I knew I'd miss her a lot, that it would be really terrible in the house without her, but if I'd had an idea it would be anything like as bad as this, that I'd feel so unbearably—'

Marjorie did not say. In her mind, sometimes, at nights, she stacked up all the furniture in the house against her daughter's departure, sharpening the locks and greasing the door-handles – but it wasn't a joke, it was the worst thing in her life.

Bette carried on speaking gently and Marjorie watched her lips forming careful letter sounds. Her own face was burning, her eyes narrowed, and finally she pressed her chin into her chest and felt a little salty stain soaking into the scooped neckline of her dress. 'I know it's bloody awful for you. But you've done the right thing, I do admire you, and I'm sure it will help things in the long run. It's just a question of being patient until things start to improve. And what else could you have done, apart from lock her up?'

'Crossed my mind,' Marjorie did not answer.

'I've thought about it so much, and what I think is, just now your interests are just a bit too close for you both to be able to see them for what they are.'

May was so self-contained, so poised and private, with her neat piles of pastel-hued stationery and her folded, colour-coded T-shirts and well-considered softly voiced opinions. Even the way her clothes draped loosely over her body was so elegant until you realised the margins were all wrong. Those clothes were intended to be form-fitting, figure-hugging garments. 'All I ever wanted was for her to feel like a huge asset to my life, a boon, a colossal blessing. What I always felt was that I'd rather be dead than have her feel in the way.'

When the Braintrees walked into her little consulting room on Monday morning it was immediately clear that the atmosphere between them was hugely altered. Something of importance had occurred. Mark shot Marjorie a glance that was so direct it almost broke something. Marjorie braced herself. She had the sense of an ending.

Helen began the talk. She spoke haltingly, and there was something automatic and rehearsed about her choice of words. Drained of colour, her face looked years younger – and she was dressed, unusually for her, in very tight clothes, so you could not help but notice her extreme narrowness and the protrusion of bone over width, which, coupled with height, gave her the air of an adolescent girl, her limbs awkward and embarrassed by the space they claimed. Her hands made sharp little flinching movements while she spoke, as though repeatedly stung, thought Marjorie.

'You see, there's been a bit of a development.'

'Development? You hardly need to dress it up. You make it sound interesting.' Mark Braintree sighed seriously, but not before Marjorie had registered the hint of a smirk on his lips. Helen saw it too. 'I suppose it's all rather embarrassing,' he muttered, with the suggestion of a shrug but no actual movement.

A week after returning from their honeymoon, out of panic and a sense of his own languid unworthiness – or was it just the envelopment by this strange new state, he wondered, because, after all, he pointed out, he had said all along – there had been witnesses – that he was unsure how being married would affect him; 'Anyhow', Mark Braintree had taken his secretary out for a four-hour lunch and ended up having, 'and there's no nice way of saying this', sex with her in an upper room of a Gower Street hotel. Helen's prying eyes had discovered the tryst's cost on an old credit-card slip last night and it had all come out. Helen was livid, of course. 'Not that that's at all unusual,' was what Mark Braintree said. 'In fact, it sounds mean-spirited, possibly, but I almost wonder whether she prefers having a concrete reason to be really angry with me rather than just that latent seething. You see, she's got the high ground now, hasn't she? And there's always a certain amount of satisfaction in that.'

There was triumph in his voice as he spoke. His cheeks had reddened and there was a sense of exhilaration. Marjorie did not quite understand – and then, suddenly, Mark began to catalogue his own suffering. 'However bad Helen might feel, I know I feel worse about this. I wouldn't expect her to see this, necessarily, but it is true. I've been thinking about what it all means and what I've concluded is this: something inside me needed to risk sabotaging the marriage, possibly because I don't feel up to it. I can't say. It may be that I'm just not ready to make the commitment, that I couldn't really be attracted to someone who was attracted to me. I'm just trying out ideas, I haven't really thought it through, but you know what I mean. It's all right for you because you're so much better than me. Obviously I'm a piece of shit compared to you.' He smiled thinly at Helen. 'The stupid thing is she wasn't even attractive, Jean wasn't. Isn't. It was just a natural outpouring of sympathy on my part. Misplaced, I don't deny. But she took the news of the wedding to heart – to her it was a terrible defection. It really meant nothing. Surely you can see that. She's barely attractive, saggy skin and hard bony arms, which is bad luck on her part because it's usually one or the other, isn't it? Or not? And I do think the lack of real attraction, that that's important. I couldn't even tell you her eye colour. It sounds foolish but I felt obliged, as a sort of kindness to a lonely woman who had taken her boss's nuptials as a blow. She's not even had a kiss in six years. I see now it was more complicated than that. That it's something I did against myself, unconsciously. But do I really have to spend the rest of my life making it up to everybody? For God's sake, I might have been unfaithful but I really wasn't disloyal. Surely you see that?'

Helen was reeling as if from a body blow: her neck had folded into her shoulders and her head hung low. Her teeth were chattering, even though the weather was mild and the room, if anything, was slightly overheated.

For some minutes everything was silent.

'I find myself wondering what you are feeling just now, Helen,' Marjorie said very, very gently.

'You don't want to know,' Helen's husband whispered, as a sort of dramatic aside.

'Will you try to tell us?'

Without raising her head Helen murmured, 'I feel like someone is trying to – to murder me and I can't—' Then she slumped further into her chair as if the effort involved in saying things was more than she could bear.

'Can't?' Marjorie prompted, after a while, but Helen could or would not speak.

Marjorie took a breath. Something very important was happening. She needed to concentrate hard, because it might be possible to make use of it.

'I wonder how you feel, Mark, when Helen says it's as though someone has tried to kill her.'

'She's so theatrical. You know, her mother was an actress before she married. Not that I'm trying to excuse myself but really! One thing I do know is this. It's something I've read, actually. Often when − what shall we call it? − *infidelity* takes place, both partners have it in mind but the one who acts first is just the person who's presented with the opportunity. It's quite a well-documented phenomenon. And it just happens that I got in there first, if you see what I mean. Not that pleasure or anything of that sort had a part to play, not from my side, I mean.' There was a flash recurrence of the smirk.

And then, suddenly, although there was a full twenty minutes remaining, Helen stood up. 'I'm really, really sorry,' she said. 'I don't mean to be rude but I just think I might just − if that's all right—' and without waiting for an answer she had passed through the door, her hands fluttering apologetically, and soon there was not even the slightest sound of her feet in the passage.

Mark Braintree gave Marjorie a long look and raised his left eyebrow, in what she felt he considered a winning manner. She assumed he would follow his wife, but he was stretching out his legs and clearing his throat. What he was doing, it gradually dawned on her, was − well, he was just getting into his stride. Perhaps this was what was needed. After a few moments, Marjorie furnished him with her least amazing smile.

'What d'you make of all this?' he asked abruptly, as though barking an order. 'What d'you make of what I've done, of what I've said? If I may ask. Or aren't you allowed to give an opinion? I expect you're not, but I imagine there are things on your mind. You're married yourself, of course? I know you won't answer that but I notice you wear a ring. I wouldn't have thought you were the marrying type. It's none of my business, of course, but there's something about you that already seems . . . How can I put this delicately? Sort of doubled. I don't just mean your size, it's more a question of style, balance or something. But I must say, last night when I couldn't sleep I found myself thinking, I wonder what he's like, your husband. Expect you keep him firmly under your thumb. Of course, one wouldn't dare get on the wrong side of you. A large fellow, I thought, or otherwise an invalid with nerves, possibly, maybe some kind of illness, one of the emotional ones. With twitches, or twinges or whatever. Or maybe there's been some sort of mild disgrace.'

Marjorie took a shallow breath and tried to enter into his picture of her pale romance.

Mark Braintree took up his thread again, his confidence increasing. His talk grew wilder – a bit of swagger here, there some cursory regret. He scrutinised her person and sighed. 'Helen's never had much in the bosom department.' He nodded appreciatively in Marjorie's direction. 'My parents didn't have any time for me, of course. Army baby and all that.'

Marjorie tried out something in her mind: 'I'm not quite sure where you're going when you say all these things. It's striking to me that your wife just walked off as a result of things you said, and yet you haven't mentioned it.' But she said nothing. It was too early to make any sort of intervention. She did not know where this was leading. Besides, in the last few seconds he had said more than he had in any of the previous seventeen sessions and she did not want to stem his flow. Well, she did and she didn't.

Now Mark Braintree's tone was speculative, enquiring. 'Sometimes I think if I never sleep with Helen again that it wouldn't bother me at all. It might actually be a relief. And then I think, well, it would certainly bother me if

I never had sex again and Helen is my wife, so . . . do
you see?'

'Are you saying having a good sexual relationship is important to you and that would be one possible reason for trying
to continue with the marriage?'

'Well, I don't want to be wasteful. And it does simplify
things.'

'Simplify?'

'I mean, finding someone else and so on.'

'Finding someone else would be . . .'

'Well, it would be a bore.'

'You almost feel it would be worth staying with Helen
because it would be easier than having to find a new partner?'

'I think that's right. And I do so hate change.' Marjorie
watched his hands, elegantly crossed at the wrists, and his long
fingers, which made unconscious touch-typing movements on
his knees. Was it a message he was transmitting, she wondered.
Did he actually know the keys?

She turned to him gently. 'You know, I'm very struck by
the language you're using. It does seem very defensive. You
say you want to try to save the marriage, but at the same
time you're suggesting that you'd like to do so because any
alternative seems too much like hard work.'

'Well, I suppose that's the long and short of it.'

'How do you think Helen would react to what you're
telling me?'

'Hysterically, perhaps.' Here he sniggered. 'I think one of
our problems is I've never really minded too much about
all the fine-tuning of her feelings. No one could any
sense of it. She's so irrational. I've never considered her inner

life my affair. I've always thought it unwise to get involved. D'you see?'

Marjorie looked straight into his eyes. 'I'm wondering what you think of the fact that she walked out of here a few moments ago. I'm conscious that you haven't referred to it.'

'Well, if she wants to make brash gestures . . .'

'Brash gestures?'

'Storming out, sulking, throwing all the toys out of the pram.'

'Do you really think she stormed out? It seemed to me that she just withdrew.'

'That's what she always does. Sometimes she's so diffident it's actually aggressive.'

'In what way aggressive?'

'Well, there's so much reporach in everything she does.'

'And what do you understand about the nature of the reproach?'

He shook his head, and the gesture had a sort of stale, bored finality to it. 'That really is her affair.'

The word hovered in the air between them like a huge beacon.

'I can't help noticing that you've used the word "affair" twice in the last couple of minutes.'

'To call it an affair is a bit of an over-investment, wouldn't you say?'

'What would you call it?'

'I don't choose to call it anything.'

'You sound quite combative as we're speaking. I wonder what you're feeling right now.'

'Oh, I don't generally go in for feelings. Leave that to

Helen. I feel pretty much the same all the time. Occasionally I feel slightly worse, but there's mainly just one mood. One key, rather.'

Marjorie took a gamble. 'That's something that someone who was feeling quite depressed might say.'

'Possibly. But what I'm wondering is this: you see, you sit here with your tactful little questions and your cautious little armchair interpretations and suggestions, and "It seems" and "It sounds like" and I really think, you know, you're probably an intelligent person. Perhaps you are. I presume you have your own kind of intelligence. Granted, you're obviously not the most disciplined person in the world – you like a degree of excess – but, then, that's not a crime. But what I don't understand is this: is it stimulating to you somehow to watch us fall apart? Does it give you a thrill to be able to go back to Roger or Brian or whoever, with his limp or his shakes or whatever it is he's got, and say. "There but for the grace of God!" Does hearing about other people's sterile embraces make you feel superior? Or do you envy us, because . . . because it's been such a long time? And either way don't you feel a bit dirtied by it all? Do we all sicken you, rather? God, you're smug sitting there.' Mark gave a little bow, raised his eyebrow again, inclined his head sharply for emphasis and sat back in his chair, recomposing his limbs and his features in an attitude that suggested he was the mildest person ever to have trodden God's earth.

'Goodness, what a lot of questions. I'm not quite sure where to start. For example, I'm very struck that you say you don't go in for feelings and yet you're almost shouting at me and your face has coloured quite deeply.'

'I've never shouted at a woman in my life. What would be the point?'

'Indeed! I wonder what has made you so angry all of a sudden. Can you try to think about it with me?'

'I must say I find your attitude incredible! This really isn't about me, you know.'

'I can see that it seems that way. And I'll happily explain one or two things about my professional outlook, if it will make you feel more confident. But only briefly, because it may be an unhelpful distraction. I choose to work as a marriage counsellor because I believe in the institution of marriage. I feel almost as though I am employed by marriage, that I work for marriage, that I treat each marriage, rather than the individuals within it, as my patients. I'm ambitious about happiness. I think a good marriage can be extremely life-affirming, a positive partnership in which individuals can blossom and become most fully themselves. It can have a sort of transforming potential. Be an environment in which old wounds can be healed and talents can be nursed, where people can learn what it means to be completely human at the very deepest level. I think being a good parent is the most valuable job in the world. If a mother can teach—'

'You see, I've never been one for that kind of talk.'

'No. I can appreciate that. We've got a bit distracted but what I wanted to say was, I wonder why you've chosen today to mention for the first time that you were an army baby and that your parents did not have any time for you – and precisely at the point that your wife walked out of the session?'

'Want to make something of it?'

'What do you make of it?'

'Have you any idea how grating your voice is? Its tonality. Its shrill pitch. Have other people said that to you? Rather a blow to be built like an opera singer and have the squeak of a church mouse I'd imagine.'

Marjorie said nothing.

'I really don't know what you've got to feel *so* superior about, I must say.'

A minute passed in silence.

'What you probably can't see is that this inflated notion you have of yourself, it's absolutely ludicrous. Like the most banal sort of television. Only worse, because you just go on and on and on and there's no end to it. There's no switching off. And then it's barely worth listening because almost everything you say is completely divorced from intelligence or truth – or common sense, even. Not to mention excruciatingly banal.'

'You already said that,' Marjorie did not say. Instead, as she had been advised in her training when there was aggression from a client, she relaxed her body posture and avoided making any eye-contact, which might be seen as provocative.

'You're so cheap and predictable.' Mark Braintree snorted.

'You sound very disappointed in me.'

Mark Braintree snorted again.

'Moments ago you sounded almost mournful when you talked about your parents not having time for you, just after your wife left the room. It seems you feel that nobody has got what you want and need.'

'Well – yes,' Mark said, and he looked up at Marjorie thoughtfully. His expression had altered and his voice had become smaller and more melancholy. 'I know I'm a shit. Obviously. Sometimes I feel like there are these three little grains of poison inside me and unless I can gouge them out I'm just going to contaminate everything I come into contact with. I've always felt like that.'

'And why do you think you see *three* grains?'

'Someone like you would say one each for my parents and one for me.'

'Yes, someone like me might well think that,' Marjorie agreed quietly, with a smile.

'I've never been any good at saying sorry.'

'Does it feel important to be good at it, rather than just to do it?'

'I don't know. Sometimes I think I'd like to learn.'

'To learn how to apologise properly?'

'How to do it at all. I suppose, to learn how to be sorry as much as say it. To feel it, to act it – I don't mean act as in pretend . . .'

'I suppose that to feel it would mean accepting you have the power to cause hurt and with that—'

'With that would come responsibilities.'

'They might well, yes.'

They sat silently together in Marjorie's room for a further five minutes, each exhausted after the little battle, the sound of their breathing punctuated by the clock's smooth ticking, the traffic braking and accelerating in the street outside.

'Well,' he glanced down at his watch, 'I see we're out of time.'

'Yes, we are, but perhaps we can continue this next time, with your wife. It feels valuable. Very much worth pursuing.'

'I was afraid you might think that.' He got up. ''Bye,' he said. 'Thanks very much.' And then an amazing thing happened. For the first time since he had come into her life Mark Braintree released a shy smile.

Marjorie was thrilled. It was not the sense of liking it conveyed that cheered her exactly: more, it was she had felt herself so strangely frayed at the seams of late and suddenly something was knitting together inside her, something springy, something resilient.

She checked herself almost immediately. Oh, no, you don't, she thought. Was this feeling a little carnivorous? Was she feeding from another's dependency? Richard Adler, her boss, an extraordinarily kind and intelligent man, encouraged his staff to make this sort of regular self-check and self-balance. 'People are going to put their hearts in your hands over and over again,' he counselled. 'Unless you fully recognise that you are probably the sort of person who needs to see the hearts of others the consequences will be destructive.'

(On their honeymoon, in the white clapboard seaside hotel, Marjorie's husband had watched her eating a large dish of peach crumble with clotted cream and said, fondly, that it was like the nicest kind of cannibalism.)

Twelve minutes later Audrey rang through to say her next clients had arrived.

They brought into the room with them an atmosphere of well-reasoned calm. The wife was small and freckled, with a sensible, cheerful outlook. The husband, who last session had seemed quite raw at the edges, today appeared almost confident: certainly, some element of his personality had started working more smoothly in his favour, Marjorie thought. A slightly built alcoholic, who was prone to depression, he had not had a drink in forty days. It was their second session. They took their seats. Marjorie let out a smile.

No one spoke. After three minutes of silence, Marjorie said, 'I'm wondering how the last week went for you both.'

'Well!' the wife said humorously. And suddenly the composure that had marked their entrance evaporated. It exploded. Jane Brint was distraught, hissing, 'At least when he was drinking he was fun. The life of the party. There was a bit of backbone. But now it feels like he hasn't just given up the drink, he's given up altogether. Living. He reads these books all day long. He says it's for his recovery. But they're not making him think straight. He's getting obsessed. It's like a cult. They telephone all hours of the day and night and he'll drop everything, just like that. Last weekend he was helping someone move house. From Friday afternoon until Sunday morning. Seven trips in the car. My car. And we can't go to my sister's wedding because there's going to be drinks around and he doesn't feel "safe". My own sister's wedding! How can that be right? And he's so serious now. Morose. Nothing's a joke. I feel like I felt when my dad died. I did everything for him. Even took him to the toilet at the end. It wasn't easy for either of us. I was only fifteen. It was a lot of responsibility. I used to lie on the floor next to his bed until he fell asleep. I had to wake him up when he stopped breathing. To lose your dad to cancer at forty-two. Four hundred people came to the funeral. I know Mike's done well with his drinking but I don't know how much more I can take. We used to have such a laugh all the time. It was one long party. The flat was always full.'

'You sound like you miss those days.'

'I don't know. I know you've done well with the drinking,

knocking it on the head, but – one minute it's a twenty-four-hour party and now everything's so quiet. He never says anything. Goes for days without speaking. And the people he hangs round with. They're so weird. He's got nothing in common. Plus he's out running five mornings a week and at night it's meetings, and it's not just the meetings it's the coffees after, and there's always someone in trouble who needs dropping home, and they always live way out and by the time he's home it's eleven o'clock and I'm just sitting indoors, worrying something awful's happening. I might as well be single for all I see of him.'

'Does it feel as though Mike's putting everything into his recovery and you're right at the bottom of the list?'

'I'm not even on the list, love. I'm not even on the list.' She started cackling hysterically in her seat. She leant forward, inclining her head for the sake of candour. 'I don't know why I'm laughing.' She had the giggles in a quite terrifying manner, her whole body quivering and her mouth bizarrely hooped with mirth. 'Whole thing makes me feel like a fucking useless cunt, if you must know!'

The room went quiet. When the worst sort of insults came flying they were almost always self-dealt. Marjorie felt a surge of sadness, like nausea, thickening in her throat. 'Mike, I notice you've been very quiet all this time. I wonder what you think about what Jane's been saying?'

'I don't know.'

'She seems to be feeling the effects of your treatment as a kind of bereavement.'

'All I know is I'm doing my best. I've got to keep my head down. It's only another few weeks and then maybe I can ease

off a bit. But it's too early for me now. I've got to be selfish
a little bit longer. I'm sorry, but I need you to bear with me.
I know I've got a lot of making up to do. But I am doing
my best.'

He turned to Marjorie. 'Everyone else thinks I'm doing well.
Eight weeks ago I was lying in the gutter outside our flats in
a pool of vomit, no job, a load of bills on the table, and the
doctor gave me six months to live, two years tops—'

'Well, you were a lot more fun to be with then.'

Marjorie blinked and caught her top lip in her teeth. Why
did change always seem to feel like betrayal?

Before they left the pair agreed that they needed to spend
more time together and suggested to each other, while Marjorie
looked on with well-concealed delight, that they make time for
at least two outings the following week, one to a local Italian
restaurant called Pizza Romantica, which was unlicensed and
situated at the end of their street, the other a walk to a park they
both liked, where they had met and where there was a small
rose garden. They were both highly stimulated by the prospect
of these dates, 'Why couldn't we think of that at home?' they
laughed, and when they left Marjorie's room a large part of
the combative atmosphere generated within the session, for the
time being at any rate, seemed to have cleared.

Marjorie left the Centre and began the twelve-minute walk
home. Dimly she thought of the Crofts in *Persuasion*. They were
people to whom her heart turned very naturally. The Admiral
and his wife, unfailingly glad of each other, striding across the
grounds at Kellynch hand in hand, brisk, warm, inseparable.
She accompanied him on all his voyages, fifteen years' worth,
feeling more seasick without him at home in Deal, unsure what

she was meant to be doing, waiting for news – be it good or ill – than she had ever done aboard ship. And for him the idea of separation was unthinkable, a real evil.

Gradually Marjorie became aware that, behind her, a woman and her giggly daughter were trying to overtake and she slowed to let them pass. The daughter was extremely fair, her head in the afternoon sunshine a dazzling flash of white and pink and gold. The woman was handsome, with an elaborate hair-style and glossy, claret-coloured lips. They seemed delighted together, egging each other on to some daring task, nudging, smiling, partners in crime. As they veered out in front of her the mother caught Marjorie's eye and smiled attractively, shyly, mouthing the words 'Hello, dear.' Marjorie smiled back, and then something extraordinary happened: the younger woman came forward with a pen and a pink-and-white spiralbound book. 'It is you, isn't it? Can I have your autograph, please?' she asked.

Marjorie examined the girl's face, which was completely unlined. She looked like a sort of beautiful fool. 'Can you *what*?'

The girl thrust the book into Marjorie's hands. 'We saw you last night. You were so right not to go home with Dr Hardy. He'd be such a pain. Mum says you can do so much better, and she should know because within a year of the divorce— He'd wear you down, he wouldn't be enough for you, make you old before your time, and you wouldn't be happy – and, anyway, Mum thinks you're still carrying a torch for Mike and it's early days and you're still on the rebound and everything.' She stopped to take a breath.

'I'm so sorry but I think you must be mixing me up with someone else.'

The girl did not seem to hear her. Then her mother approached. 'Sally has a bit of a problem separating reality from fiction. I do hope we're not troubling you but we couldn't resist saying hello. I do apologise if, you know, we've sprung at you out of the blue. Please don't ever think that we don't respect your privacy. We just couldn't resist.'

The young girl was talking again: 'We're all crazy about *Nightingale Park* in my class. I've been watching it since I was seven years old.'

'It's true, she has. Of course, it's had its fallow years but it's really picked up again these last weeks, since you came on to the ward. In fact, you're our best thing.' She smiled ironically. 'I mean Rose Dempsey, your character. It's so wonderful to see someone who is a good person on the television.' She hesitated. 'I don't mean bland. I don't mean boring. What's the right word? Someone relatable-to, is what I'm trying to say. Rose Dempsey is what I'm like on a good day.'

'You wish, Mum!'

'Don't be so mean.'

'In your dreams.'

'Honestly! Do you have children — in real life, I mean? I know Rose may not be able to because of complications after the . . . the operation but—'

'Do you know? It's funny, but I haven't the faintest idea what you're talking about.'

'What?'

'I simply don't know what you're talking about. Rose

Dempsey and everything. Dr Hardy. Complications. You've made a mistake. I've no idea what you're talking about.'

'Well, I think that's very rude.'

'I'm sorry, but I don't know what else to say.'

'Well, you could at least—'

'I'm afraid you've muddled me up with someone else.'

'Come on, Sally. If she wants to play mind games, that's fine! I'm really sorry we inconvenienced you. But it's false economy, dear, if you want to know what I think, putting on these silly airs. And you're not doing yourself any favours either because, before you know it, you'll be yesterday's chip paper, begging people to recognise you in the street and they just won't want to know.' She snorted and turned away, taking her daughter harshly by the hand. 'Let's face it, dear, you're hardly the National Shakespeare Company, are you, now?'

'Stuck-up cow!' Sally was heard to whisper under her breath. 'Two-bit soap has-been.'

'Wow,' Marjorie murmured quietly, amazed by this sudden flash of asperity.

After a minute's thought, Marjorie relented. The older woman, twenty yards ahead, was already browsing in a nearby dress shop but the daughter was outside, dawdling grumpily, peering at the taupe-coloured pleated skirts in the window, tugging at the waistband of her underwear through the fabric of her low-rise jeans. All of a sudden Marjorie burst into view. 'Excuse me!' She greeted the young girl brightly with her highest voltage smile. 'I'm so sorry. I owe you a huge apology. I'm having one of those days. You know what it's like. I'd forget my head if it wasn't tied on. I had a late night and I don't know if I'm coming or going. I'd love to sign your book. I didn't get to sleep until the small hours. Say you'll forgive me?'

'Were you at the soap awards?'

'Er – that's no excuse for rudeness, though. Do forgive me. I'm a ball of shame! And I'd love to sign your book. Shall I put "To Sally"? I feel terrible about this.' She slipped a bangle off her arm and handed it to the girl. 'Can I give you this, as a sorry?'

She scrawled an unreadable signature next to a warm message of good wishes.

'Thanks,' the girl said casually, but as Marjorie continued up the street a high-pitched hysterical wail stopped her in her tracks: 'Mum! Quick! Look! Look! Mum! *Mum!* She signed the book and I think it's REAL SILVER!'

A smile crept over Marjorie's face, brightening her eyes, which she blinked and settled into an inquisitive, alluring gaze. She altered her gait to one that was at once more celebratory and poised. Was it Rose Dempsey's walk, she wondered. She tried to picture the character in her mind's eye. She was comely and decent certainly, that much had been established. But was her childlessness something she wore lightly? Was it an affliction? You couldn't help wondering.

She would phone up May when she got home and tell her all about it. Only she had spoken to her daughter two days earlier and you could not just bombard people with phone calls. She would save it up for their next meeting, perhaps. A little sparkling anecdote to break the ice.

When Marjorie returned home she saw her lodger, Frank,

struggling down the narrow basement steps with a large black plastic sack, which was how he liked to transport his washing back from the launderette. The bag was grazed where it had rubbed against the wall and threatening to split, and Frank himself was jammed into the small railinged opening that was scarcely big enough for a person, let alone three loads of washing. He smiled wearily. 'Marjorie,' he said, buffeting the bag with his knees.

'Frank,' she replied. He was on the bottom step now, looking up at her, clutching the sack to his body awkwardly while attempting to locate his keys. 'Do you ever watch television?' she asked.

'I don't have one,' he replied. 'Don't have anything against them in principle, though,' he added hurriedly.

'Oh.'

'Why d'you ask?'

'Oh. No reason.'

He looked vastly disappointed. 'Do you think they're a good invention on the whole? Or not? Hard to say, I expect,' he gabbled. 'I'll give it a bit more thought. I mustn't keep you, must I?' His voice slowed suddenly with regret.

Then, to her utmost surprise, Marjorie heard her voice say: 'Twist your arm and invite you in for a cup of tea, or are you in the middle of things?'

'No. Nothing that couldn't wait. In fact, why not come to me? I've got rather a fine packet of biscuits that could do with being opened. I don't mean it's about to reach its expiry date, it's nowhere near, in fact. I was just saving them for . . . I mean . . . You must think I sound so pathetic.'

'Thank you very much,' Marjorie said, and followed him down the stairs to his flat. It was dark there and smelt of greens, but the biscuits were exceptional, she told him. She would remember them. But Frank did not answer, he just muttered bashfully into his shoulder, his eyes low and his narrow face reddening wildly.

Nightingale Park, according to Marjorie's evening paper, was on that very evening at six forty-five. In fact, it was featured in the Pick of the Day column. *Is Dr Hardy about to make Rose an offer she can't refuse?*

At the appointed hour Marjorie unzipped her chocolate-coloured knee boots and made herself comfortable in one of Hugh's old jerseys. There were Sleeptight and two grapefruits on a tray on her lap. As the credits rolled she absently unravelled a little wool from her left cuff, smoothing the dry kinks out of the grey merino, and peered intently at the TV set.

The scene opened in a large London teaching hospital. Uniformed porters were hurtling a young woman on a trolley down a brightly lit corridor, as though she were a bowling ball, with much shouting and flapping of arms. In the corner of the picture three nurses were huddled together with their backs to the camera, their rounded, feminine shoulders suggesting secrets. Just then the dark one swung round to reprimand the porters for their carelessness. Marjorie gasped and gripped her chair. 'No!' she said. 'OH, MY GOD!' It was *her*: a mirror image or a photograph, only more real, as though she were seeing herself as a nurse in her dreams. The physical match was so startling that Marjorie laughed out loud and clutched at her ribs. The thicker upper portion balanced on slender foundations, like a tulip-shaped sundae glass. The hair with the chestnut glints. The full mouth. The suggestion of both good sense and excess in the large green eyes, the frank lips, the hips that were one part private hula-hula girl and two parts childbearing. Yet Rose Dempsey wore her fleshy sensuality lightly. That is, she did not appear to have any sort of attitude towards it. It was certainly no encumbrance. How did you manage that? It was very well done.

Within minutes it was clear that Rose Dempsey was the moral backbone of the show. A divorcée, childless, with a penchant for tortoiseshell hair accessories, she was as crisp and proper as her sky-blue staff nurse's uniform. At weekends she probably indulged in wholesome pursuits, such as rambling and building confidence through play at a local children's home. At work she dispensed advice to all comers. Grateful patients showered her with chocolates and flowers. She was the heroine of the neo-natal unit: hardworking, intuitive, obliging. At the beginning of this episode a baby's ecstatic parents named their daughter Rose after her. Tender feelings were blossoming in Marjorie. Rose was genuinely inspiring. 'You're a wonderful star!' Marjorie mouthed at the television, watching her lips form the words against the darkness of the consultant's pinstripes outside the operating theatre on the screen. Of course, she had her weaknesses like anyone else, her blind spots. She could be awkward at times, snappy when overtired or shy or a little naïve. It was wrong to set these people up too high, but nevertheless . . . She was so unfailingly likeable. Discreet and sensible by day, she did not entirely lack glamour after hours. Under their starched apron her legs in sheer stockings were shapely, her lips rarely unenhanced. The soul of discretion, she was party to everyone's secrets. But all along there were quite unsubtle hints that Rose had secrets of her own.

Three

The following day after work Marjorie paid her daughter a surprise visit, as she did every Tuesday, bringing with her a selection of the necessities of life — bread, butter, cheese, milk, sausages, spaghetti and chocolate biscuits, fruit, cleaning fluids, bath things, the opaque black tights May wore and, because it was that time in the month, some sanitary protection.

May was newly installed in a tiny student flat with three tiny girls from college who worked in a coffee bar in the evenings and were never at home. Each Tuesday mother and daughter spent their designated hour together, May delivering a continuous stream of tea and college gossip, swathed in her strange assortment of loose pyjama tops and crumpled sports clothes, while Marjorie looked on encouragingly.

Marjorie rattled the knocker and called, 'Are you decent?' through the letterbox.

'OK OK OK.' May's voice was waspish and exasperated. 'I'm on the phone!'

'Don't rush. I've got my book!' Marjorie drew a pale blue

volume entitled *Rethinking Marriage for the New Millennium* out of her bag, and settled herself on the doorstep, carefully arranging the folds of her cassis-coloured skirt around her to avoid unnecessary creasing. After six minutes May came to the door.

'Are you in the middle of things, rather? I'm so sorry. Shall I pop back in half an hour? I could easily go and find myself a bit of something. I'm sorry I called at such a bad time.'

'No, it's OK.' May's lips wore an expression of sealed defeat. 'I'm really sorry I kept you waiting.'

'Oh, no! That's really totally OK. It's always great to have an extra free minute to oneself anyway. Not that—'

May led her mother along the hall and down the narrow staircase into the gloomy basement living room. 'I'll put the kettle on, shall I?'

'Ooh, yes, please.' Marjorie took a seat. 'I could go murdering for a cup!' she mumbled. Was that an expression? Was it near enough? While May tended the kettle Marjorie took an inventory of the items on the coffee-table. Next to a neat pile of textbooks was a metallic blue propelling pencil, a cardboard box containing some free trial sachets of face cream, six hairgrips, a cinema-ticket stub and three purple foil and Cellophane sweet wrappers, which (if Marjorie was not mistaken) had formerly clothed hazelnuts suspended in caramel and enrobed in thick milk chocolate. At the other end of the table there was a rust-brown apple core and a half-eaten jar of baby food. On the label a fluffy lamb gambolled across a landscape of carrots and swede. 'Need any help?'

May returned with a tray, shaking her head. 'How's work?' she asked.

'Oh, you know. Just as you think people are past the worst some awful new development crops up, but then other couples who you're really worried about start getting on and none of us has any idea why, but of course we hardly like to question it.' Marjorie spoke a little dreamily. 'You know, I've got all the time in the world for people who are in a muddle and who are doing everything they can to try to improve things.' She checked herself, then carried on, more cautiously, 'That's not to say I've no patience with those who find it harder to . . . I know it can be impossible sometimes. I try not to judge. But I am often genuinely moved by the efforts people make to do what doesn't really come naturally. The lengths they're prepared to go to to make things work.'

'You take it all so personally.'

'How else would I take it?'

'I suppose.'

'Anyway. Anyway.' *Be more upbeat can't you?* Marjorie self-instructed. 'You'll never guess what happened yesterday. I'm walking down the street minding my own business – well, sort of, as much as I'm able, you know it's not my strongest card – and some woman, well, two women start chasing after me and then, out of the blue, they ask for my autograph.'

'No!'

'It's true, yes, because it just so happens I bear a striking resemblance to one of our major stars of stage and screen. Rose Dempsey from some television programme called *Nightingale Court*. D'you know it?'

'*Nightingale Park*. Haven't seen it for years but Trish loves that show.'

'Well, I'm the moral linchpin of the whole thing, apparently.

Good in a crisis, dependable, hard-working. Not that I've seen it, you understand – well, just once. The thing is, it's a busy time for me, as far as I can tell. I may be up for promotion next week, and it's possible that wedding bells could be ringing in the background. If you really want to know.'

May clinked her teacup against her mother's. 'That's good news!'

'Oh, you're welcome. So, anyway, I gave them my autograph, even though I didn't know what I was meant to be writing. I just scribbled a couple of lines that could be anything and off they went, happy as sandboys, and off I went as well. *So!* Eve Rice, I think she's called.'

'Who is?'

'The actress who plays my character. Eve Rice,' Marjorie rolled the name round her mouth. She took several sips of her tea and refilled her cup from the pot. 'You know, it's not too bad, as these things go. Some of the dialogue seems a bit stilted but a lot of the arguing is really well done.'

May smiled. 'You know it's on four nights a week?'

'No, just Mondays, I think.'

'I'm telling you it's on Monday, Wednesday, Friday and Sunday, all at six forty-five apart from Wednesday when it's on at nine forty-five because of the football. I know, because Trish tries to organise her shifts round it.'

'I am going to be busy!'

May made more tea. She was squinting oddly at her mother, as though through a camera lens. 'I guess you'll have to get yourself some sort of disguise or something.'

'What a good idea.' Absently Marjorie dipped a teaspoon into her tea – it was her fifth cup – and pressed the warm, milky steel to her cheek. 'Curly wig, d'you think? Wraparound sunglasses? Snakeskin boots?'

'That would certainly help you melt into the crowd!'

'You know, she's an awfully nice woman. There's something about her, a sort of moral quality that isn't at all dreary, quite the reverse, and she seems to bring such a lightness of touch to everything. The way she goes about things. I'm not explaining this at all well. You'll have to tune in. Do let me know what you think, won't you?'

May laughed.

'I know. I know. You don't have to tell me I'm a fool.' Marjorie was flushed with pleasure and it took more than a minute for the smile on her mouth to fade. She closed her eyes briefly. When she opened them May was gazing out of the front window, which gave on to a yellowish brick wall, looking very slightly melancholy. Marjorie tried out some lines in her mind. 'Is everything OK, darling?' No, that was *hopeless*. 'All well with you?' Too breezy. 'How's it going?' Possibly – that was what May said to her friends on the telephone. Her daughter was looking at her intently now.

'Mum?'

'Yes, darling?'

'There's something I wanted to ask you. It might sound a bit mad, but you know when couples come to see you and it's because the wife really wants to patch things up, is pretending that there's still a chance but really both know it's over and the husband is just going through the motions, trying to keep the peace, to please her, and sort of privately to get tips on how to separate efficiently?'

'Ye-es . . . I think I know what you mean, although there are always two sides to these things, I must say.'

'That's what I was wondering. I mean, do you think it's possible that, almost without wanting to or meaning to, during the process a couple who had really given up on each other might realise that things could still work out, almost despite themselves, then decide to make a go of things, even if they hadn't both embarked on the whole thing with much hope or intentions or anything? It's a friend of mine's mum and dad, and she doesn't quite know what to hope for. What d'you think?'

'Oh dear. That is sad. Poor old thing.'

'Yeah, I know. But could it just kind of creep up on them, a solution, a reconciliation, even, if one side wasn't really looking for it? Because of the process. That's what she's wondering. She's pretty sure her dad's given up trying but—'

'Well, I suppose two things spring to mind. Sometimes a man will tell himself and those around him that he's agreed to counselling just because his spouse has requested it, or because he thinks it will make things look better in court. He may think counselling is a waste of time, or a show of weakness, or it might just be a very frightening process to him – or for his own pride he may not wish to be seen to have initiated it, but in fact it may be that, deep down, he is genuinely interested and relieved to begin counselling, and actually puts a lot of work into trying to sort things out, sometimes with success. Or it could be that the man genuinely agrees to do the counselling to placate his wife or prove to her that the relationship really is over, but as the sessions progress he discovers important insights about himself that make his own life and sense of self, and therefore the relationship, seem more manageable, more attractive, even when it wasn't necessarily his initial intention to stay with it. So she shouldn't give up hope entirely, your friend.'

'Oh, thanks, I'll tell her.' May looked dully away.

'Have I somehow said the wrong . . .' Marjorie thought a little more. 'When there's a third party involved, of course, things get more complicated, as you would expect.' Was that going too far?

'Of course.'

'Is that helpful, at all?'

'Yeah, no – I mean, I'll mull it over and try to explain.'

'If you wanted me to talk about it further to your friend, if you thought that was appropriate, I suppose I . . . ?' Marjorie had no idea what, exactly, she was offering but—

'No, it'll be fine. Thanks, though.'

'Not at all.'

'Want some more tea?'

'Go on, then. What's with the baby food?' Marjorie asked, highly casually.

'Oh, some friend of Trish's left it here by mistake, she's got a baby of about eight weeks and I tried a bit, out of boredom mainly. Those babies don't know they're born. It's delicious. A hundred per cent organic.'

Marjorie thought carefully before she spoke. It was unclear what she was dealing with, but she did not want mad risks. 'I know I'm not meant to interfere but I think this is important. An eight-week-old baby shouldn't really be on solids, especially not meat. It's dangerous. They don't have the digestive system to cope. I hope you don't mind my saying.'

'Did I say eight weeks? I meant eight months. That's OK, isn't it?'

'What a relief. That's a perfectly balanced meal for a child of that age. I'm so sorry. I was beginning to feel quite anxious for a moment.'

'Mum!'

'Anyway, here's your shopping.' Marjorie swiftly handed May the bags full of groceries. As always, a crisp ten-pound note was Sellotaped to the underside of the packet of biscuits.

'Great,' May said.

'Your friend with the baby, does she have a man in her life?'

'It's all really complicated, but basically – no.'

'Are the grandparents around?'

'Not really. They live abroad so—'

'Poor thing. Do tell her if she ever wants a babysitter, I'd be happy to help. I bet she could do with a break now and then.'

'Thanks. That's really kind.'

Just then the telephone rang. May grabbed at it and turned away to a dark corner by the window, her eyes fixed intently on her shoes.

'Shall I make myself scarce?' Marjorie scribbled rapidly on a scrap of paper, but she did not know how to get it to May on the other side of the room.

'Oh,' May was saying, 'you again.' Her voice was hard.

There were levels of disappointment in it that Marjorie was horrified to hear.

'I knew it was going to be something like that,' May said. She dropped her voice and curved her body in on itself, her head leaning on the wall, her back to Marjorie. 'I just think . . . Look, I can't talk now. I'll phone you back. OK, you call then.' Without saying goodbye May hung up.

Marjorie glanced at her watch. 'Everything OK?' she mumbled.

'Oh, yeah. Just the usual old rubbish!' May said cheerily. 'Men!'

'Oh, I know!' Marjorie said, although as soon as she spoke the words she felt old, immature, clumsy, ridiculous and a fool.

May gave her a funny look.

'From work, I mean.' Marjorie clarified her position. 'Of course, women are just as bad. And as good!' she added. It was true.

'Right', May said, biting her lip, amused.

'Oh, you know what I mean. Take no notice!'

One of May's childhood games:

Marjorie: Hello [speaking into a banana]. It's the lady from the cake shop here. You got friends for tea?

May: Yes. Friends for tea.

Marjorie: Shall I deliver some cakes, dear? You want to know what we got? Well, there's strawberry shortcake and lemon tart and chocolate fudge brownies and plain cake and coffee and walnut gateau.

May: Yes yes yes. Cakes, please.

Marjorie: One of each shall I bring. They big eaters, your pals?

May: Ta. Cakes, please.

Marjorie: About four o'clock shall I pop over? That okey-dokey?

May: Okey-dokey. Bye-bye.
Marjorie: 'Bye, dear.

Marjorie glanced again at her watch. Aren't we getting on well? she thought. She began to gather up her things, absently tidying cups into the sink, rinsing them, wiping them down.

'Oh, leave that,' May said. 'I'll do it later.'

'Oh, no! What an idiot. I'm afraid it's done now. I'm so sorry.'

'It's OK. Thanks.'

'Lovely to see you, May.'

'See you soon, yeah?'

'See you.'

Marjorie wandered over to the door. She could not stand these partings, but she knew that to linger would be wrong. She opened it and peered out into the street where two black cats were scrapping viciously at the kerbside over a small triangle of orange peel. She looked back at May and then she just could not help herself: 'May, you are eating enough, aren't you?'

'Mum!'

'I am sorry, but you look like you're slipping away. I know I'm not meant to mention it but—'

'For God's sake!' May was stern, her small rosebud mouth a hateful pink dot.

'It's just there's nothing to you.'

'Mum!'

'I'm sorry, I'm sorry.'

'I should think so.'

74

'It's just that . . .'

'I know.'

'Please don't be angry with me.'

'I'm not angry with you. You just drive me crazy, that's all.'

'I suppose I can live with that.'

'Yeah, well – I'm sure *you* can.'

'I really am sorry, May.'

'It's all right. Just, you know – you always make everything so much worse.'

'I know. I'll get out of your hair. I really am sorry. I'll see you next week.'

'You know what? Maybe we should leave it for a week or two.'

Marjorie felt a huge blunt weight strike her and took two sideways steps uncertainly. Her eyes were stinging but she smiled reasonably. She took her punishment. 'All right, if you like to. That's fine. I'll give a ring in a fortnight or so, shall I?' and with that she let herself calmly out. 'Thank you for all that lovely tea,' she called to her daughter, but the front door was already firmly shut.

Five months earlier Marjorie had been passing dishes to May through the serving-hatch in the ground-floor back kitchen. The table was laid in the front room with an embroidered cloth and a bunch of daffodils in a green-glazed vase. It was Sunday lunch. A sacred family time. There was a plate of roast meat and some creamy potato gratin in a shallow earthenware pot, some cauliflower in white sauce, a bowl of cabbage and bacon, some carrots done with Parmesan and a steaming jug of gravy. A green salad dressed with lemon juice and snipped chives brought up the rear. Behind the scenes, out of sight in the kitchen, a quivering trifle lurked, its wonky layers of yellow, pink and white sinking slowly into each other.

'Wish I was more hungry,' May said nervously.

'You break my heart saying things like that,' Marjorie replied, smiling. 'Shall I pass you the salad, then?'

May put some green leaves on her plate. After a while she added a slice of meat. She ate extremely slowly, laying down her knife and fork between each mouthful.

'Potatoes?'

'I'm all right for the minute.'

'Is it cold out?' Marjorie enquired gently.

'Not as bad as it looks.'

'That's what I thought but, then, the weather forecast said . . .' Marjorie chatted on brightly, while May ate at a snail's pace. 'It's the first day of spring today . . . well, officially it is, but looking at the rain . . . It's the kind of day that my mother used to describe as "disgusting". She always took the weather so personally. It was mad, really.' Marjorie did not allow her gaze to fall on her daughter's plate. You're doing well, she said to herself. You're doing well. What May wanted to eat was her own affair. Of course it was. It was good to be healthy. Not everyone wanted to spend Sunday afternoon deeply entrenched in a food coma.

The sum of May's food intake so far was exactly three lettuce leaves and two square inches of meat. May took up her cutlery again and Marjorie tried to relax, but after a while May placed it at the side of her plate, again without seeming to notice she had not taken any more mouthfuls. It was excruciating. Marjorie did not know how not to take it as a slight. She was trying, though, using up great rusty reserves of cheer. She smiled. 'Is that a new T-shirt?' she asked. 'They have such beautiful things now.' She prised some crispy potato morsels from the lip of the dish, not looking at her daughter as she spoke. And now May's cutlery lay neatly across her plate. It was definitely all over. Thing was, she'd put so much love into the food. On to Marjorie's plate ('Just have a little taste of everything') tears were falling swiftly. 'I just can't bear it,' she did not say. She lifted herself out of her chair, very gradually, as though she might change her mind at any moment and take a milder form of action. She thought of putting herself in another room until the feelings passed. She needed to cool down: her throat was dry and sore, thick with all her unuttered thoughts. But it wasn't possible to continue. I'm trying. I am trying, she thought, but before she knew it, afraid of what she might say or do, she had run out into the street and up to the main road, and the rain turned into hail and the hail turned into huge grey gobbets of snow. As she was in her cardigan, she walked into a burger bar, because it was the nearest thing, and took her place in the longest queue, and each time she neared the front she ducked away to the back again, and after a while a mannish elderly woman, with white wisps of hair on her chin, saw that she was crying and ushered Marjorie to one side, where there was some kind of red and yellow plastic train that was intended for children to sit in while they ate their food, and they took their tiny seats in the nearest carriage where the older lady held her hand and said, 'What's the matter, pet?' and her Scottish accent was so strong that Marjorie could barely understand her.

Marjorie opened her mouth to wail, 'My . . . daughter won't

eat her lunch and I can't bear it,' but what came out was a huge, choking sob and 'My husband's died and I don't know what to do!'

The woman grabbed her arm athletically and said, 'You have a good cry, pet. Go on! Go on!' She urged. She insisted. 'Do you the world of good.' She clasped Marjorie by the shoulders and was shaking her. 'He was a good man, then, eh, pet?' Marjorie nodded. 'That's the way.' The woman agreed sagely. 'Mine's still with us, you know. But, then, I never cared for him so much. Bit too free with his fists. So . . .' Her voice trailed off sadly. 'So . . .'

Marjorie stopped crying. The play train stank of greased meat and stale chips and (was it?) dirty nappies, and there were great smears of oil on the little red awning that separated the compartments from the driver's section, and some starchy-looking fruits-of-the-forest pie filling had somehow attached itself to Marjorie's shoe.

The woman was talking wildly: 'Sometimes I've thought about killing him, if you'd like to know!'

'Really?'

'When he's laying there at midnight, reeking and snoring, I've thought, Do it now. Do it *now.*'

'How would you do it? Smother him with a pillow?'

'Argh, I've no' the nerve, pet. I've no' the nerve. Ye have to laugh, really! Your angel of a man's dead as a doorpost and there's my rotter with not a scratch an' me wishin' him six foot underground.'

'I know,' Marjorie said. 'That's very like life, isn't it?'

'You telling me, darling! You telling me! You had no luck finding a replacement for him, pet, your man?'

'No. I haven't really got the energy. I've got my work and my daughter's seventeen now so, so—'

'She courting?'

'She doesn't tell me anything like that. I think there's someone but—'

'No, well, that's the way of it now. They like their independence. Except on washday and when you've got cash in your hands.'

'I know.'

'You'll be OK, pet. You're like me. It hits you hard, but you get through it. Ah can tell.'

'Thanks.'

'You go home to your daughter now. Have you no umbrella?'

'No, but I'm only round the corner.'

'Did you wan' some chips before you go?'

'Thanks.' Marjorie put what she was offered into her mouth.

'Take some back for your daughter, then, p'raps?'

'No, er, no. She only likes health food. You know these teenagers and their fads.'

'Well, I'm here if you need me,' the woman said. 'And I'll no' be charging for advice! 'Bye, lamb. Take care of y'self just now.'

'Thanks. 'Bye.'

''Bye now. 'Bye now. 'Bye-ee.'

Marjorie walked back into the house. May was watching television and reading a book with the radio on. She had cleared the food off the table and into the kitchen.

She had covered Marjorie's plate with a bowl.

'I'm so sorry, darling.'

'No, it's me, I'm sorry.'

'You know I love you, don't you?'

'Yes, I do.'

'I'm just scared of losing you I – don't know if—'

'But you won't lose me.'

'No?'

'No. I will always, always, always—'

But Marjorie had flown into her daughter's arms and her own were wrapped round May so tightly that there was no space for words. May's hair was in her mouth, and she could feel the heat of their love moistening her neck and her underarms and the spaces inside her elbows. After a minute or two May loosened the embrace. 'There is something I need to tell you, though, Mum. I was going to tell you at lunchtime.'

'Oh?' she said. Here it comes. She braced herself.

'Me and three of the girls from college have found a little flat up the road. It's cheap – a bargain – and you can visit the whole time, and I do think it's for the best, Mum. In the long run. We'll probably see more of each other than we do now.'

'Yes, darling. You're so sensible and right.' Marjorie was nodding and smiling, nodding and smiling. Her throat was raw. 'It's probably for the best.' She clenched the inside of her cheeks with her back teeth. Don't say anything else. Just don't say anything. Don't say anything, she repeated, over and over, in her brain, smiling and nodding for dear life.

Of course she had seen it all coming. She used to pad about the upper floors at night-time when she knew the end was near, sometimes dragging a pillow off her bed and positioning herself outside May's room, listening acutely for night breaths, for movement, for signs or clues to her life. May was a good sleeper now. Marjorie folded her hands under her head like a picture of a woman in repose but her mind was racing with wild promises and resolutions and bargaining. She knew that what she was practising was a species of invasion but she did not know how to retreat. What she thought was, Marjorie, this just isn't good. She rubbed her thumbs hard against each other till a small patch of skin wore away.

Through the black chink in the door she heard May's body stirring or shifting minutely and, although it was pitch dark, she peered in and looked towards the dark rectangle where she knew her daughter lay. Suddenly she felt herself wholly incapable of innocent thoughts: 'Just give me a few more weeks,' she whispered to herself, 'just one more Christmas. Don't let her go without a few more pounds.' Marjorie nursed a genuine fear that, out of her clutches, May might absolutely dwindle and disappear.

For a second Marjorie saw a future bloated with non-events. She tried to swallow, but her throat was dry and sour. She wanted to wake her daughter and list to May her star qualities over and over again until she believed them all. 'You have been unfailingly lovely, always, really,' she wanted to say. 'Even to know you is a vast privilege, let alone to be your mother.' She spoke out the words. 'I cannot bear it if you leave. It will kill me.' May's breaths were solid and even. They calmed Marjorie slightly. I don't seem to torment you when you're asleep is one good thing, Marjorie thought. I don't get on her nerves. We're just spending time together while we still can. We're just two people. We're only human. I'm sure we're both doing our best. She tried to seem resigned, but something in her reeled wildly, for any second now would bring on the end. She felt the bleak exhilaration of a person newly bankrupt. Nothing to lose now! Nothing left worth losing!

She returned to her own bed and dreamed without sleeping, day-dreams, protracted wonderings: a stab of insult, a crescent-moon smile taken the wrong way – misinterpreted as sarcasm – a disapproving frown that proved the last straw. All the nights seemed to pass in continual rainstorms. She heard water running down the walls of the house, beating on the flat slate roof. On the day of Hugh's funeral people had called the drizzly weather appropriate, but she had wanted the morning filled with sun. She had lipsticked her lips and, in her soot-coloured coat, she had kicked furiously at the raked piles of dead leaves.

She imagined May in her bed and rehearsed out loud the items in her daughter's room – walls, curtains, shelves, red wool rug, desk, bed, two chairs. She saw May climbing into her blue-and-white nightclothes, raspberry pink from her bath. She placed a kiss on her face and smoothed down her hair.

Marjorie fell asleep, murmuring under her breath. It was quite incredible that May was gone suddenly. If only there were some sort of permanent familiar insight she could draw on, but all her thoughts would say was, 'Look, haven't you had this feeling before?'

The next morning Marjorie had her fortnightly supervision with Richard Adler, the Centre's director. 'How are the Braintrees coming along?' he asked.

Marjorie shook her head. 'They're not a brilliant advertisement for me, I must say.'

'Hmmm?' Richard said, after some consideration.

'Often it seems as though they hardly like each other at all. There is so much anger and disappointment on both sides. They're so set in their ways. It's almost as though they've decided between them that he'll be distant and aloof because that's what he thinks men do – it's what his father did – and she'll suffer and seethe because that's what she thinks women do. In some ways they're quite clear about it, and his mother was just like Helen, from what I gather, and she grew up without a father but with rather a cool mother who didn't have time for her and— They seem to consider the unsatisfactory patterns they've got into to be so inevitable.'

'It sounds very frustrating.'

'It is. Very.'

'And how do you see your role?'

'I think if they both felt the other one was really listening attentively to what they had to say, listening a hundred per cent, then it would mean an awful lot. They do love each other hugely, more than they realise, I'm sure. They're definitely in it for the long haul. They just need to find ways of showing it better. They play a lot of games with each other, but the games get so hurtful and they don't realise how they affect the other. I think if he listened to her acutely for even twenty minutes, now and then, but regularly, and made her feel important, unchallenged, intelligent and valuable, and if she did the same a few times a week, it could make a world of difference.'

Richard nodded.

'I'm going to try to work towards that in the next session.'

Richard nodded again. 'Can I ask you something?'

'Of course.'

'It worries me slightly when you say that the Braintrees are not a good advertisement for you.'

'Well, you know, I feel I ought to have moved them beyond this point by now.'

'How do you mean exactly?'

'Well, I had hoped that by this stage they would be happier with each other, surer of how to live. More content. More settled.'

'It can be awfully disappointing when progress is slow.'

'I just wish I could get through to them more. Help them realise that the difficulties they have are really quite surmountable, if I can only get them to—'

'Have you considered that the difficulties they have might not be surmountable?'

'Don't!'

'It does happen.'

'I really don't think so in this case. I've just got to try harder. Try different things. Get them to as well. I just have this feeling that if we can only strip everything away, all the projections and the muddling and things, the patterns . . . Because it always seems to me that the unconscious – when left to its own devices, deep down, when you strip all the rubbish away – that in the end, really, it is a force for health. If you think about it. That's my experience, anyway.'

'Explain a bit more.'

'Well, when you really think about it. I know if I can just encourage – or allow them to allow themselves – to come into their own that everything will get much better. If they can somehow have the confidence to really be themselves at the deepest level. Be a bit fearless, maybe. Really open things up to the best possible outcome.' Surely that could not be her shrill voice that was throbbing through the room? 'Please don't think I've got my head in the sand. I'm not trivialising their difficulties. I mean . . . I'll read you my notes from the last session. "The Braintrees are stuck and I'm starting to think it suits them. They say things out loud, but it isn't really any sort of a conversation. Self-dramatising tone – some of which seems to be for effect. Possibly playing with fire, not sure. Two options. (1) They need to do some proper work, make some kind of commitment to changing things Or (B), I mean (2) Must decide to accept themselves as they are."'

'It's a bit striking that you don't consider separation to be any kind of option for them.'

'Well, it's not—'

'Even though I know, from what you've said before, that it's a subject that regularly comes up during their sessions.'

'They're never serious about it, though. Not really. I mean, they may sound as though they are, they use it to make drama, but – surely we're all just trying to . . . I mean . . . Everyone knows . . .' She stopped speaking.

Richard was looking warmly at her. Marjorie relaxed her body in the light of his smile. 'I'm not disagreeing with you. Please don't think that. All I'm saying is that it's good to hold the whole picture in your mind. Otherwise one becomes so . . . I don't know . . . vulnerable, I suppose.' Marjorie nodded. 'Let's move on, shall we? What about the new referral, the recovering alcoholic and his wife?'

'Oh.' Marjorie flicked through her folder to find their notes. 'It's a bit sticky now, but I'm pretty sure they'll be fine too. In the end.'

Richard raised an eyebrow.

'There's an awful lot of work to do but I've got a good feeling. A good feeling that we'll all be able to work together well. I mean, they're both very good at expressing themselves, at articulating their thoughts and feelings – that's what I'm trying to say, if you see what I mean. It's very promising. In that way.'

Richard nodded at her seriously. His shirt was of soft powder-blue cotton and when you looked very closely you could just make out a fine herringbone pattern in the fabric. 'I hope you don't think I'm speaking out of turn. I know how conscientious you are, how committed you are to the work we do here. It's just, in the past few months, you've seemed a little distracted. A little less rigorous, more emotional in yourself, less certain of things, of your bearings, of your aims, than you used to be. It's not exactly a question of confidence. If anything, it's a matter of emphasis. It's hard to explain what it is and perhaps I'm overstating things. It might be my mistake – or, rather, not so much a mistake, more an exaggeration. On my part, that is. But I must confess that I find myself feeling a little worried about you and I feel I need to tell you. I suppose what I'm trying to ask you is this.' Here he dropped his voice. 'Is everything all right?'

Straight away Marjorie nodded crisply. A door slammed further along the corridor and she imagined May exiting the building, dragging behind her an enormous suitcase on minuscule wheels. 'Fine, fine, fine,' she said. 'Really. Never better. But I will take your points on – on board.' For a second she wanted to carry on this seafaring theme, shout something madcap and vaguely stripy such as 'Anchors aweigh!'

or 'Man the rigging!', but, of course, she did not say these things. Instead she smiled sweetly and made fluttering feminine movements with her fingertips across the starched cotton piqué of her blouse.

Richard was looking at her thoughtfully. She could not quite grasp what his fears were. Was he afraid that her – what were they? – *organs* of concern were shrivelling up? Did she seem like the woman who'd been treated mercilessly at the training because she considered candlelit dinners and frilly underwear to be a cure-all? Did he think she was losing her mind?

Richard was speaking again: 'Can I come back to the Braintrees for a moment?

'Of course.'

'I get the impression that in some way they're getting to you in a way that they haven't before. And I suppose I wonder if you'd like to think about that with me.'

'Oh, you know what I'm like. Take no notice. Please!' Marjorie laughed, and bit her lip, but the laugh had sounded more hollow than she'd anticipated and somehow graceless.

'Can I tell you something, Marjorie?' Richard spoke lightly. 'It's just something rather lovely that happened at the weekend. Victoria and I went on a retreat – I think I mentioned it to you. It was in the Lake District and, rather uniquely, it was for couples who both work in the caring professions, mainly doctors, it transpired. Anyway, the theme for the weekend was how to be a family. We were asked to look at the ideas we'd had about our own birth families before getting married and starting new families of our own. There was a lot of talk about how both partners carry their own ideas about family life into the new partnership although the ideas, the rituals, the beliefs, may be very different, may even clash. And then, right in the middle of it, Victoria and I had *the* most extraordinary conversation. Completely out of the blue. And – I hope this doesn't sound terrible – it was really a little bit life-affirming.'

Marjorie, hugely intrigued, smiled warmly and tried to arrange her features into the mildest sort of a question mark. Richard took a short, serious breath and began to speak as though telling a story: 'At the time that we married, Victoria and I were both extremely clear about our . . . I suppose you'd call them our beginnings. I came from a family where everything was very open. Everything was discussed. There wasn't anything you couldn't say at the kitchen table. My parents encouraged us to talk freely about anything and everything. It was part of our family consciousness. Something we took pride in. We weren't the types to brush things under the carpet. Nothing was taboo in our open, liberal household. It was almost a boast.

'Victoria's family, you see, was exactly the opposite. They talked a little about what was for dinner, but they didn't express themselves as we did. It's not that they were repressed, exactly, it's just that they were cautious and reserved about a number of things. As people often are. It's something we've often thought about together. Anyway, while we were talking at the weekend, in a small group with some others who were examining similar issues, we realised that this was a misleading way of looking at things. After all this time, it dawned on us that we were being partially sighted about the whole thing because in my family, for all our openness and free-talking, nothing ever got done. Nothing changed. We would talk about a problem or a difference of opinion till we were blue in the face, but we never did anything about it. So all that talking was essentially a conservative thing. It gave us the illusion that we were all rather dynamic but its function was the opposite – all it did was ensure there was no change. Victoria's family, although much more restrained, on the rare occasion when something difficult was discussed action was taken, usually immediately. Things changed. People sat up and noticed what was said and did something about it straight away. So the ideas we'd been carrying around about ourselves, although not the opposite of the truth, were really only half-truths – less than half, perhaps.'

Marjorie nodded.

'D'you see what I mean?'

Marjorie nodded again, although she was not entirely sure that she did.

Four

At three minutes to twelve Audrey was on the intercom to say that Marjorie's new clients had arrived. They were seven minutes late. Marjorie put down her book, inserting a tortoiseshell hair-slide as a marker half-way through a chapter called 'Fidelity as a Moral Achievement'. It had been dawn before she had got herself off to sleep.

Jim and Barbara Henshaw wandered into her room slowly and quietly, as though afraid they might be disturbing something. Barbara seemed shaky, all her movements nervous and unsure. She had been waiting for Jim in the car park behind the Centre, in a freak rainstorm, for twenty minutes: she was shivering now and her long red hair was wet and hung in thickly matted curtains round her face.

'I wish you'd just gone in without me. I feel terrible,' Jim was saying. 'D'you want my jersey? Shall I put your coat on the radiator?'

'Oh, don't worry.'

'I'm so sorry. I hope you don't catch a chill.' He drew off his navy jumper and passed it to his wife.

'Thanks,' she said and, without looking up, she put the garment on.

Jim looked morose, his shoulders tensed under a huge weight of care. 'It's me who wanted to come,' he said. 'I feel that Barbara isn't happy and I don't know how to make it better. And I wondered . . . I wondered if you might be able to help us. At all.'

Barbara's chin was glued to her chest, her shoulders were curled in, her legs so tightly crossed that, through her tights, you could see her foot leaving a long pink welt on her shin.

'I'm afraid – and I hope you don't mind me saying this, darling, but I'm afraid she seems to be crying an awful lot. Especially in the mornings when I go off to work. I wonder if it might be some kind of separation anxiety. You see, her parents travelled widely when she was a child and we both feel it's made her extra sensitive to, you know, comings and goings.

'Thing is, I can't really not go to work. I'd love to stay with her but, you know, we need the money and so on. I feel a brute walking out on her. I can see her trying to be so brave, but everything seems so painful for her. I don't know what to do. I wonder if she might be depressed.'

Barbara shifted in her seat, but her face was still well hidden.

'I wonder what you both feel is making you sad, Barbara?'

'You see, when I ask her if there's anything she's unhappy about, she just says she loves her life and she's got everything she wants. If there was something wrong I could put right or change or arrange differently . . .'

'Barbara's unhappiness sounds extremely painful for you also.'

'I don't mind about that, I just want her to feel better. I've tried arranging a few things to colour in her days a bit. My younger sister, whom she likes, comes round one or two mornings a week, and on Wednesday afternoon she has a weekly aromatherapy massage, and her nieces come to play after school on Thursday. If she feels up to it. And I've arranged things at work so I leave home at nine and get home at six, which is about as short a day as I can get away with, and I don't really know what else to do.'

'You sound despairing, Jim.'

'I feel such a failure, which I know is selfish in itself and I'm not proud of it. But I'll do anything you say. You see, I'm trying so hard to keep everything together. I know I've got to be strong for Barbara, but I'm just not sure if—'

It was clear from the quivering of her back that, hunched in her seat, Barbara was crying now. Her shoulders were making regular flinching movements. Marjorie wanted to address her, but her hidden face and obvious distress seemed so defensive that it felt as though putting any question to her, even of the mildest sort, when she had gone to such pains to remove herself from the realm of the conversation, would be a form of assault. Still, Marjorie felt it was something that needed acknowledgement.

'Barbara, I can see you're in pain and I'm wondering if there is any way that you might feel able to put anything about . . . about what you're feeling into words. If you can allow us to try to help you.'

Barbara's head sank into her knees and suddenly, with a rapid alarmed jolt, she covered it with both her arms, as though she were about to be attacked from above.

Marjorie watched Barbara's distress strike Jim's face like a
fist. His mouth gaped open and, for a second, it seemed that
a wide, agonised howl was about to come, only no sound was
emitted. His eyes streamed tears. Then his shoulders heaved
with despair, he clutched his ribs, and it seemed he was
mumbling something between noiseless sobs, which Marjorie
could not hear. Soon it became apparent. Over and over he
was saying, 'Please tell me what to do . . . Please tell me
what to do. We'll do whatever it takes. Please help us. Please
help us . . .'

Then Barbara let out a long, high wailing noise. It was
an extraordinary sound. Barbara herself seemed amazed. Her
whole body was shaking, and then something broke and they
sat there, the pair of them, sobbing hysterically, so entirely
convulsed with their mysterious grief that Marjorie felt the
walls of the small consulting room smarting with their misery.
Rapidly it grew hot and airless. Outside, some slender birds
circled wildly against the smudged clouds. Ten minutes passed
in this fashion and the quality of the couple's sadness grew so
deep and high and sheer that Marjorie found herself regarding
it with the highest admiration.

They've got each other, Marjorie said gently to herself. It
made the whole thing completely bearable. They have got
each other. And they've got me. She wished she was their
friend and not their counsellor, in which case she would allow
herself to say, 'With some hard work I know for certain that,
in time, things will become much easier for you,' because she
believed that this was the case with all her heart. And just at
that moment Jim went over to Barbara's seat and folded her
in his arms, rocking her gently to and fro. Something in the

room had given: there was a sense of a loosening and, for an instant, Marjorie wanted to join them, take their hands, tell them how brave they were to let go of themselves like this in front of a virtual stranger. All sorts of tributes sprang to her lips – what an honour it was for her to be in the company of people who were prepared to experience their deepest feelings so honestly, how it took some couples years to reach this point of no return from which (astonishingly) some kind of return was almost always the most striking consequence. Marjorie put her hand to her chin so that her fingers covered her mouth. She wished she could make them some kind of definitive, saving pronouncement such as – she stumbled over it in her mind, but something like, 'You see, the thing is love makes truth bearable and, really, it's truth that makes love possible.' But it was not her place. She bit her lip and instead she just thought these thoughts as solidly as she was able, hoping that her concentration might permit her fellow-feeling to bleed in some measure into the consciousness of this couple as they sat weeping in her little room for the best part of an hour.

In the windowless staff room at the Centre, there was a cream plastic jug kettle, discoloured round the lip, and a cupboard with a wood-effect Formica counter and a sink and a mug tree and a willow-pattern tea caddy and four collapsible white resin chairs. David Phillips, Marjorie's most senior colleague, was standing, thoughtfully, waiting for the water to come to the boil. 'All right?' He half laughed, his face glowing unhealthily under the fluorescent lighting strip. His saw-toothed smile was disconcerting. Possibly he considered her ridiculous.

'Why are you laughing?' Marjorie asked.

'Oh, no reason. All well?'

She nodded. 'And you?'

'Could be worse. Decree nisi coming through next week, so . . . ?'

Marjorie paused. 'Does that feel . . . ?'

'Let the celebrating begin, I say.'

'Oh!' She busied herself with rinsing out a cup that was stained inside with thickly caked rings of tea. She applied a soapy cloth.

He tutted. 'Marjorie, Marjorie, Marjorie!' he said.

'What?' She straightened herself abruptly, jutting her chin into the air.

'You know something? Sometimes, not always but sometimes, and it's not specially unusual, I might just add, when a marriage ends it can be a good thing. A great thing, in some cases. Often, in fact.'

Marjorie sucked her lip. She sighed.

'Well?' he said.

She sniffed and imagined a thin piece of wire pulling her nose, shoulders and torso upwards. Finally, she swung her head round to face him. 'Is that a fact?' She walked off quietly, leaving her colleague wincing as he fished a boiling teabag out of his cup with a crooked finger. What she might have said, only it would have been a shade unfair, was 'When your husband's in the graveyard it puts a rather different complexion on things. Do you see?' She pictured the shadowy corner beneath the lime tree. The marriage had been virtually stillborn. The dead little scenes, lit from behind. The day she had come home with May from the hospital he had hung pleated muslin at all the windows to surprise her. 'A feminine touch!' he said. The mackintosh and sturdy walking-shoes they had purchased together for her to wear on honeymoon when it had rained incessantly – how had he known? He made her put on his thick socks indoors, after their walks, to ward off colds. He had scratched the soles of her shoes with scissor points so that she would not slip. With Hugh you were in the presence of intelligence. His guesses were so good. 'What animal has the highest blood pressure?' the board-game quiz card asked. 'A giraffe, perhaps? Of course!' They would not be 'scenes' now in her memory, were he still alive. When people asked, she said, 'It's just a very dull ache now, that's all.' The tree was ancient and thriving. It was a triumph for it to have him just there.

That evening May and Marjorie went to the cinema. With some merriment and stumbling, they sat down in their seats. It was excessively warm and dark in the red plush room, with its steep incline, and Marjorie felt a sense of peace, a sense of achievement, her face and upper body obscured by a sixteen-inch carton of sugared popcorn. She barely looked at the film: it was something extra-terrestrial, something May had chosen, of no interest whatsoever to her mother, but Marjorie was enjoying her daughter's company enormously. Their knees were scarcely a foot apart. She smiled indulgently and ate several handfuls of popcorn in quick succession. It was like being lovesick teenagers. She gazed contentedly at the edge of May's head. Her hair was still soft, like a baby's. She felt madcap and a little extreme. What kind of enterprise had they embarked on?

May's ears had such an elegant shape to them. Really, they were little works of art. Marjorie turned away, her gaze fearful of discovery. On the screen, a space princess was having her toes painted a bronze colour by a robot beautician. She wished she could find better ways to manage and administer their mother–daughter communion. She knew the struggles May had to keep on loving. She saw that for her daughter it was all a business of heavy responsibilities whereas to Marjorie it was huge privileges all the way. 'Well, that's hardly fair,' she murmured, under her breath. 'That's not fair at all.' Who was she to enjoy all the lightness? But how to effect a rebalance? Was that even an expression?

The cinema had been May's idea. 'A way of being together and a bit separate at the same time,' she had not quite said. 'You know, of being free and easy with each other again.' That was what she had meant, surely? A kind of loosening of pressure around the fracture, around the dislocation, until some new alignment was able to take.

May was so intelligent and sensible it could break your heart. Marjorie was ashamed that her daughter had to offer such suggestions, but May was right: it *was* happy-making, being out together in public at the pictures. Why not?

May was fidgeting in her seat, trying to take off her jacket without standing, and then, when that had been achieved, she stretched out her arms to remove another garment, and then another and another, with the minimum of fuss.

'Isn't it boiling?' Marjorie chuckled.

'What? Oh, yeah.'

'Shall I get you a drink?'

'No, it's fine.'

'Have some popcorn.'

'What? Sssssh.'

Suddenly the screen brightened as the action moved to the luminous white-and-silver upper floor of the enemy's space capsule, flooding the auditorium with light. Marjorie gasped; May's private nude arms were as stiff and narrow as iris leaves. Even absorbed in the dextrous task of splitting a frayed end of her hair right back to the root, which was how May liked to relax, the joints seemed raw and ill-aligned. The light was ghoulish and unnatural, but even still . . .

'Have some popcorn.' Marjorie set the carton carefully on May's knees, her own arms trembling.

May returned it promptly. 'I can't take all that. It's way too much.'

About a third of the carton spilled on to the lap of Marjorie's brown tweed fishtail skirt. She felt a tear burning in her eye as she gathered up the kernels and allowed them to soften in her mouth. That was what people said at the end of love, wasn't it? You did one last thing, played out some final saving gamble, and they said, *No, I can't take any more, it's too much what you ask.* And then they went. And what was the end of love, exactly? It wasn't death because it could keep going despite that. No, in a funny way that made it easier. There was no wear and tear. That wasn't it. But was it a mother lurking outside her daughter's empty room in the middle of the night, sleepless, guilty-proud, in the hope of catching some breathing sounds when, in reality, that daughter had been gone for months and months? Was it just a physical matter, absolute separation, a thorough, for-ever unravelling of brains, veins and intestines? Bette had said, 'It'll get worse before it gets better, but it will get better in time and once it's better – you'll be amazed.' But Marjorie did not want to be amazed. She wanted her daughter back. She did not mind their struggles. She prized them. She did not want the kind of days that were just a mindless bumping into the scenery. She did not want to live in an aquarium where all the warmth and life were separate and unreachable behind plate glass and you were expected just to watch and learn blithely and imagine what it would be to feel involved. Sometimes, it seemed, May took their meetings like a brave soul who had been condemned to a holiday of the most unwelcome sort. Still. She was doing her best. They both were, weren't they? Had it always been this way?

May's first day at school — Marjorie slumped at the school gates, weakened with a night of crying and too much coffee. She had actually thought of locking herself into the stationery cupboard or posing with a mop and an overall in the girls' loos. She loved their days spent together in the house, playing hide-and-seek and baking cakes with bearhugs and finger-paints and picnics, and cooking clay pinch-pots in the oven, and knitting and sewing outfits for May's four dollies, which were called Blue Baby, White Baby, Pink Baby and Baby Caroline, who had been named on the box by the toy company and wore a yellow matinée jacket. Should she train to be a teacher so that they could spend their days together always? Would that be mad?

Marjorie had paced the streets while May fashioned butter-flies out of cardboard and coloured pipe-cleaners, and drained a beaker of orange squash, and practised singing Christmas songs. It's good that you're well dressed, thought Marjorie. She did not look too desperate. She could have easily been between arrangements. Appointments. The time dragged cruelly. It was bitterly cold and Marjorie was lacking in defences. She drank more coffee in a café with a giraffe theme, and then another cup and another. 'This isn't suitable behaviour,' a voice in her head chided her. At break-time she retraced her steps and lingered by the playground fence, hoping to catch a glimpse of you-know-who. She would not brave the house alone. It had so many obscure regions. In the smaller bathroom on the top floor there were half-forgotten taps that had not been turned for years.

But when May raced out of school at two forty it was better than Christmas, and all the lights in Marjorie's heart came on and the funny pair danced down the street, laughing and whooping hand in hand through all the dazzling colours, running and skipping and singing wild tunes and making animal noises at the tops of their voices, and clowning about in cafés with huge slabs of cake and cocoa and ice-creams in tall sundae glasses with long spoons, and hot cuddles and rich declarations of affection flew through the air thick and fast from both sides.

Helen Braintree sat down. Straight away there was a strength to her physical presence that Marjorie had never before observed. All her gestures – the swift crossing of the legs, the clasping of the hands, the breathing, which was smooth and controlled – seemed highly defined and deliberate. At the same time there was an air of exhilaration about her.

'Look, we did try your being-nice-to-each-other idea and it lasted five, no, ten minutes. Of course, Mark's idea of getting on was just not saying anything to me at all, ignoring me completely. He brought a book to the restaurant! A biography of all things. Berlioz. Originally I had thought it would be easier to get on out of the house. The thing is, I feel he owes me an apology for what happened with Jean. I can't let it go. I know I should rise above it but I don't know how. And although he'll make excuses and give reasons et cetera, and say how it's worse for him than it is for me – he'll say he was stupid, that it's something he regrets – he refuses to say he's sorry, and until he does I just don't see how we can . . .' Here she paused and made a shallow, casual exhalation. 'What I've decided is, unless he does by the end of the week – says sorry, I mean – then I'm going to leave at the weekend.'

'Ah, the old ultimatum.' Mark's voice was dismissive but his eyes darted round the room anxiously.

'You sound as though you are very clear about your position, Helen.'

'It feels easy to be.'

'I think I can hear relief in your voice.'

'I am relieved. I know where I am.'

'What do you think when Helen says you owe her an apology?'

Mark was rubbing his thumbs against each other over and over again, occasionally separating them, then bringing them back together, forwards and back again at a surprisingly fast pace, seemingly oblivious to the rustling noise his fidgeting made. 'What I think is this: I'm sorry she feels the way she does but that's just not how apologies work. You can't demand them, they have to be given freely, and I'm afraid the more you badger me the less I feel like doing anything generous.'

'He thinks apologising to me would be some sort of precious gift.'

'Well, it obviously means a lot to her.'

Helen turned to Marjorie. 'In any normal situation he would be apologising madly and I would be saying, "I just don't know whether I can forgive you." How come we've completely bypassed that stage? I don't understand how he's swung things round. I think he's enjoying the power that withholding the apology gives him.'

'Mark?'

'I don't know about stages. But everyone knows that there's no pleasure in, say, telling someone that you love them if they keep on at you about it all day long. One needs space to let these feelings develop.'

'I can't believe this. What makes you think apologising to me should be about your own pleasure?'

'Mark, are you saying that on one level you actually do want to apologise to Helen?'

'You see, with her harping on about it endlessly, it's impossible to know what I want. Of course I'm not against the idea in principle. It's nothing like that.'

'Can we try to think for a moment what it is that's holding you back, then?'

'I just can't stand any sense of obligation.'

'How do you mean?'

'Well, I hate the feeling that anything's expected of me. I'm allergic to it. I immediately find myself wanting to do the opposite.'

'I don't go round expecting things from you all the time, but I do need to know I can count on you.'

Marjorie was impressed.

'Of course you can count on me. It's just you're always so angry. Everyone thinks you're an absolute mouse, but she flies into these giant rages at the drop of a hat. And sometimes I think you want me to behave appallingly because it makes you feel happier about being so angry and disappointed all the time.'

Helen flinched in her chair. 'I am angry,' she said. 'I am disappointed.'

'Well, there you are! You don't give me a chance. I know I do things that make you angry but I think – how can I explain? I think you were already angry. And disappointed. And you would have been angry had I done the things or not. So – so—'

'So you may as well do them anyway?' Helen barked.

'Well – almost!' Mark replied.

'It sounds to me that what you are saying, Mark, is that if Helen wasn't so angry and disappointed, you would not feel the need to behave badly.'

'Exactly.'

'Well, if you didn't behave so badly I wouldn't need to be so angry.'

'But don't you see that your anger predated me?'

'What do you think about that, Helen?'

'It's certainly true to say I had angry feelings before I met Mark. I think you'll find most people don't get to thirty-one without ever being cross with someone.'

'It's more than that, Helen,' Mark cautioned her.

'You see? He's so manipulative. He's pulled the wool over your eyes as well. We're meant to be discussing why he won't apologise and he's turned it all back on me again.'

'What do you think would happen if you said sorry, Mark?' Marjorie enquired.

'No idea.'

'It sounds as though you think you made a mistake, that you regret your actions and can see that the effects of your behaviour have been destructive. And . . . and hurtful. Would you agree?'

'I suppose so, yes.'

'And yet an apology would involve other things as well, would it? Other elements that you feel less sure of?'

'I don't know.'

'I feel it's important to try to think about it.

'Are you afraid that an apology might carry with it other obligations and you'd feel allergic to them too?'

'Possibly.'

'It's the remorse that's missing, of course.' Helen sucked at her lips. 'Notable by its absence.'

'What d'you think of that?'

'If you're going to force it out of me what I would say is this: I imagine I find it hard to say sorry because I'm not altogether sorry. Helen does things that are just about as bad almost every day.'

'When have I ever even—'

'You have such a low opinion of me for a start.'

'I love you.'

'You may love me but you don't think much of me. You make it sound as though you love me against your better judgement, despite your better self. I could start demanding apologies for that, couldn't I? Leaving my suitcase lying on the bed half packed and some threatening notes on the fridge. It's just that that's not how I choose to do things.'

Helen glared but Mark continued, his eyes flashing brilliantly,

'What you fail to grasp is, if you think so badly of me, it's rather tempting to live up to your expectations.'

'How very convenient.'

'Let's stop for a minute,' Marjorie intervened. 'I want to clarify one or two things. Helen, do you think Mark is being fair when he says you have a low opinion of him and that this is something he finds deeply upsetting, an area where he would like to see change?'

'It's news to me.'

'That's a lie!'

'But if what he says is what he truly feels, what would your response be?'

'Well, it would be that I used to think the world of him and . . . and that I'd like to again.' She broke into a smile. 'I wish he would just look at me and say, "Helen, I'm really, really sorry about what happened with Jean. It was a stupid and horrible thing to do and I regret it hugely. I was an idiot. I don't want to lose you. I'll make it up to you in any way I can. And I promise that nothing like that will ever, ever happen again."'

'So you're not only insisting I apologise, you want a hand in the wording as well.'

'All I'm saying is that if his apology is any less comprehensive, well, then, as I say, I'm going to move out for a few days at the weekend.'

'Ah – so it's just a temporary measure, then.'

'Would you like it to be more permanent?'

'Would you?'

'I asked first.'

'And I asked last.'

Helen exhaled loudly. She looked tired. They all did.

'Here we go again,' Mark commented, with a blackly comic glare.

'What's that supposed to mean?'

'You are just *so*—'

'*So* what?'

'Why do you get so angry with me?'

'I don't.'

'Oh, you do, you know you do.'

'Well, talking to you. Living with you. You don't know what it's like. It's like – it's like . . . trying to get blood into a stone.'

Silently Marjorie placed her right hand on top of the left and squeezed them together until they were pink and hot. 'It's almost time now.'

'What's our homework?' Helen enquired.

'I'd like each of you to really think of . . .' Marjorie searched her brain but could come up with nothing '. . . to give a lot of thought to – It seems we may be reaching some sort of crisis point and I think we need to reassess your commitment to the work we're doing here.'

'You sound like you want to bang our heads together,' Helen suggested.

'Believe me, it's crossed my mind,' Marjorie did not say. Instead she smiled briefly.

'I think you think our relationship is worse than it is,' Helen began brightly. 'Compared to a lot of people, you know, we do get on quite well, and neither of us is really unhappy and we do still have nice times.'

'It's not untrue what she says,' Mark conceded grudgingly.

'An awful lot of people are far more miserable than we are.'

'Are you anxious that I think you're more miserable than you are?'

'Well, sometimes you do look at Mark as though he's a beast.'

'I wonder what makes you say that.'

'She does have a point, you know.'

'Perhaps this is something we can continue with next Friday,' but it is time now.

Marjorie exited the Centre briskly, making a tight corner at the roundabout, clutching the edges of her raincoat together and flattening her hair against the wind. A leaf caught in her lapel and she tried to bat it away, but its stalk stuck in her buttonhole and its five points, which were hard and sharp, left tiny specks of dirt on her coat. She dabbed at the marks with a handkerchief. Why did people insist on living out these long plateaux of discontent, scuttling away when help or change threatened to shake things up or present them in a different light?

She dawdled at a nearby fish shop, standing in the shadow of the blue-and-white awning, admiring the handsome display. Sometimes she wondered if the Braintrees were aware of this fishmonger's, which was really among the best in London. Did they know the power of a good meal to soothe and charm? She gazed approvingly at the red and pink tilapia, the glossy metallic sea bream, the large slab of gleaming cod, which bordered a hunk of ruby tuna loin. A huge pile of scallops, in their hand-shaped half-shells, caught her eye, their corals an almost luminous orange. It was a whole different world. Behind the counter, a tanned, burly assistant hacked into an enormous turbot, forcing a saw into the bone with the heel of his hand.

Marjorie surveyed the little parade of shops, singly, calculating what each had to offer the sore at heart. The new baker's was a very average specimen, its counters stuffed with vast synthetic-cream buns and pastry-covered cheesecakes thatched with desiccated-coconut strands. She glanced at the postcard notices Sellotaped to the shop window: the carefully worded offers, in blue biro, from piano teachers and dog-walkers and part-time housekeepers and toaster vendors (new, unused, packaging complete). Why did these cards seem so touching, like the highest form of care? In the wig shop there was a sale on – 15 per cent off. In seventeen years Marjorie had never seen anyone pass through its doors. Yet something was keeping them all going. There was even a vacancy, a note in the window announced, 'Personable, mature lady or gent sought for part-time position.' Marjorie considered the word 'personable'. If you could do that, she supposed, you could do anything. In the Russian restaurant, which was expensive-looking, with soft vanilla-coloured walls and highly cushioned banquettes, one or two discreet women were seated with coffee, staring at their untouched slabs of apple cake, as if the whole business was a strain. In the evening, though, Marjorie imagined it might come into its own. It looked like a place where amends could be made. She had heard that the portions were large. Through a gap in the Roman blinds you could detect activity in the kitchen. A chef wearing headphones was preparing vegetables with a paring knife for dinner-time.

His head jigged about vaguely as he mouthed the words of the music, and his knife rose and fell with a certain rhythm. He was slender for a cook, with matted dark curly hair. Just then he looked up and caught Marjorie's gaze. He stared at her for a few moments, then waved at her and she managed to lip-read the words, 'My mum loves you.' She did a double thumbs-up and briskly withdrew.

She imagined the Braintrees having dinner there, Mark clutching his Berlioz biography and Helen seething quietly in her Paisley dress. Marjorie quickened her pace. Outside the Swedish grocer, which had a huge crispbread promotion running, Marjorie spied a beaming man, late thirties, perhaps, with a confident gait, wearing a lightweight herringbone coat, talking animatedly on a mobile telephone. 'So you keep saying,' he remarked into thin air, a flirtatious note creeping into his voice, his head inclined, eyes humorous and dark-lashed and intent. 'So you keep saying,' he announced again. Beneath the handsome coat he wore a green tie with a ridged texture and a pale grey shirt. The colour combination made her think of Babar. Peering closer Marjorie noticed that his right-hand sleeve hung loose and empty. The man was missing an arm. She stared at the brave place where the arm should have been until the man caught her gaze and made a dismissive little scowl. Marjorie was mortified. She mouthed, 'Sorry,' in his direction, and scuttled away, shame hunching her shoulders and reddening her cheeks. In her embarrassment she ran straight into a pair of 'fans' with autograph books cocked, their pages sharp against her cold fingers, the bindings square and hard-cornered. Briefly she prayed for strength. She turned away for a moment and, with a flurry of fingers and spittle, did what she could to improve her appearance. She had been practising her *Rose Dempsey*, adding a regal flourish to the R and the Y and introducing a more artistic, histrionic slant to her usual even hand. Actressy writing, she thought. The character of Rose was neatish and dependable but the actress herself – she could not quite remember the name – might be quite the reverse, fiery-tempered, a jangling bag of nerves, with an addiction to compliments and a taste for scarlet evening gowns. Who could honestly say?

She signed their books and their copies of this week's *TV Smart* (Was that too much for them to have asked? She did not know the form) and chatted animatedly for a moment before excusing herself. When people praised her performance now, her personality, or the good sense she contributed to the show, she found herself saying to them, shyly, conspiratorially, 'You know, you've really made my day.' It was possibly a little insincere – but the reactions it produced! They *reeled* with pleasure. She might as well play the game.

As she turned the corner she saw the 'So you keep saying' man again, still on the telephone, his eyes brimming with pleasure or love. Marjorie gasped. With regret, and a modicum of sadness, she saw she had been mistaken. It was quite clear the man had the full complement of limbs because the hand that wasn't cradling the phone was absently smoothing his hair.

She scurried up the street past the Gammon Rasher and the lamp shop, her eyes fixed to the ground. She paused at the pelican crossing, and when she looked up she saw her daughter staring at her neck. A man was with her. A man of average appearance wearing an unexceptional not-quite-navy-blue suit, a skinny man, pale and computerish.

'Hi, Mum,' she said. 'What's up?

'Darling, what a lovely surprise. Oh, you know. Business as usual, three steps forward two steps back. Just noting any changes in the neighbourhood. Did you see the new kite shop? Will they get enough trade, do you think?'

'Mum's a marriage-guidance counsellor,' May said to her companion, as if it were an explanation.

He broke into an uncomfortable laugh, which quickly faded into an embarrassed smile. 'Good for you,' he said finally.

'Why do you say that?' Marjorie did not ask. Instead, she smiled and nodded cordially.

'Mum, this is David. David – my mother, Marjorie.' They shook hands. David's were flabby and damp.

'Has anyone told you you look a bit like Rose Dempsey from *Nightingale Park*?'

Marjorie nodded warmly and smiled.

'It really is quite uncanny,' David said.

Marjorie laughed gently and nodded again.

'So,' David said, 'we're just off to have a drink over the road. Like to join us?'

Marjorie looked at May, who was standing behind her friend, shaking her head frantically and waving her hands from side to side. 'Another time,' she said. 'Got a lot on my plate this evening. Thanks, though.'

'See you next Tuesday, eh?' May said.

'Yes, see you then, dear. Thanks. Wonderful. I'll look forward to it. 'Bye, darling. 'Bye, Michael.'

Marjorie walked into the Russian restaurant, sucking her top lip. 'Would you do me a hot chocolate, please, extra hot?' she requested the waiter, who was gazing at her attractively.

'On the house. It is our honour!' he said, performing a little bow.

Marjorie arranged her features into one of her bashful poses. 'No, no, no,' she countered, tossing her head back graciously, with a deep smile. 'I can't allow that!'

'Madame,' the waiter leaned in so that she could smell hot peppermints on his breath, glimpse the flurry of chest hairs under his white shirt, 'the manager insists.'

What could you do?

That night Marjorie tossed and turned. May's boyfriend's wedding band throbbed in her brain, its rose-gold lustre making her throat ache. She's a sensible girl, she consoled herself. She knows what she's doing. He might be a widower, she reasoned. Unlikely but not impossible. Separated. Unfortunately some people considered themselves to be separated when they went out to work in the morning, leaving their wives at home. David Phillips, her senior colleague at work, had a favourite joke: 'Went to a wedding last week. Not sure it's going to work out though. Separate cakes.'

Marjorie got up and made herself a pot of Sleeptight tea. On the television a late-night confessional talk-show was playing. A woman said, 'I've always been sensitive. I've always hated goodbyes. Sometimes I cry when I'm putting the rubbish out because I know I'll never see it again.' And then, suddenly, the show was over and cowboys were thundering across the screen.

When May was born Hugh had been ecstatic. He did not like to be out of her sight. Her birth coincided with his annual four-week holiday, and for the first four weeks of her life May had slept in their bed at night, stretched out on her father's pale chest, her back to his front, her arms lying open to greet the world. He would not hear of a cot. He was a confident father. He read up on the subject. He knew all the winding techniques and the hygiene routines. Marjorie had told all this to May, of course. It was her favourite bedtime story. 'And how did I do my hands when I was sleeping?' she would ask, and Marjorie would demonstrate. 'And how did I do my head on Dad? Tell me again. Get me the photographs.' Marjorie fetched the heavy leather albums. 'Tell me again how I did my head, again. More. More. More.' She would do anything rather than bring May up with a big hole in her heart. 'Show me how I had my hand on the spade at the funeral. And did I wave? Did I? Did I? Did I? Aaaaaaah. Wasn't I sweet?'

The burial was not as bad as it might have been. There was an appropriate number of mourners and they were serious and well turned-out in shades of grey and dark blue. They knew the words to the hymns and their voices were sincere, woven out of the things in their hearts. Marjorie had taken pains with her dress. Her central nervous system was numbed for action by large bi-colour ovoid pills. She held May elaborately, like a bouquet, and she presented her to the guests to hold when they asked. It seemed to make them feel so good. During the ceremony May wept and someone took her outside to see the birds in the churchyard. *She must be a great comfort to you. Is she a good baby? You'll always have a bit of him. He'll live in her. She has his smile. You take care of Mum, now.* The child was screaming. Sometimes, in the middle of the night, Marjorie forgot if it was a girl or a boy.

When it came to replacing the first bit of earth over the coffin Marjorie fetched May from the person who was holding her and tucked her inside her own coat, her pink head and floppy arms peeping out from under the terrible black wool. Marjorie picked up the spade and somehow, before she realised what was going on, May's tiny fist had fixed round the handle. Marjorie had covered it with her own and then, together, they shovelled, weakly, a few spoonfuls of mud into the dark hole, which smelt of green leaves and bark. The mud was rich and damp and healthy. She wanted to say something warm, such as, 'It's just you and me now, darling' or 'The two of us', but someone was asking if she could possibly hold May again and so she gave the moment away.

'You're very lucky – you can get away with anything for the next five years!' her sister wrote. Belinda considered herself a mild person, sorely tried by circumstances. She had mad rages, learned at their mother's knee. 'I hate you. Get out of my sight!' Marjorie had had to have her tonsils removed. They were on the way back from the hospital in the car. Marjorie's throat felt like it had swallowed scissors. No one had warned her of the pain. They had talked enticingly of ice cream, but all she was given was dry toast and breakfast cereal. When they got home Marjorie climbed weakly into the bath. Her sister and her mother stood in the corner of the room their eyes transfixed by the four little rolls of flesh that comprised Marjorie's seven-year-old tummy, laughing and pointing, their faces electric with shame.

Nearly all the letters of condolence contained baby gifts. It was a strange combination: the notes bemoaning the terrible waste of a life flooded in with garish orange bean-filled tigers or red plastic shape-sorters or flabby material books, generally about families with small babies.

> *Babies are nice* [Marjorie wrote back to one acquaintance]. *They keep me busy. Oh, yes! Thanks for the corduroy piglet. May talks of little else! It is a tragic loss, of course, as you say. We are doing all right. Good days and bad days.*
> *Goodbye then,*
> *Marjorie.*

Marjorie examined the note and reprimanded herself. You can't end a letter 'Goodbye then,' she scolded. Why not? she asked back. What are you meant to do? These people who barely knew her said how happy she had made Hugh. How dare they?

Sometimes it felt as though anything anyone ever said had just been fished out of some handy local slop-bucket. She liked to gaze up at the ceiling. It was solid and it had no cracks at all. Lying in bed in one of Hugh's vast jerseys, which was hiked up round her neck, she saw May's fishy mouth sucking hard on her nipples, which were luminous little red hot bloody buds. She loved to stroke May's head. Her hair was so fine and beautiful it made Marjorie cry. She worried she might make a bald patch but the baby seemed happy so she kept on. She could not stop. A butterfly flew in through an open window and settled on the bedside table next to a coloured glass. It sat there for hours!

In the mornings, soon after dawn, she rose and wheeled May up and down Edgware Road in her pram. Slowly the street came to life: bread was baking, you could smell it everywhere, and concertinaed shop awnings were cranked down while chairs, taken off café tables after the floor had been mopped, were turned the right way up. The small queue of men and women, with mysterious white breath, outside the bank was admitted by a senior colleague entrusted with the keys. She told May about all that was going on, making little explanations when necessary. 'See that gentleman there? Well, I think he owns the jewellery shop and they also have a pawn-broker's next door, which means you can take your things and swap them for cash.' Marjorie and May and the pram wove in and out of the shops, mainly browsing and chatting about what they saw and did. She was still wearing Hugh's clothes at this time — well, his coats and scarves and shirts, not his trousers or shoes, which made her look like a clown. He had not bought new things often but when he did it was all top quality. From behind, she wondered, in his navy wool and cashmere overcoat, her hair tucked into her collar and a scarf, did she look like him a little bit? She used his softest jersey as a blanket for May. It was black and huge and covered her nicely. A slender woman passing in the street said, 'How chic to have a black baby shawl! They have such lovely things now, don't they? Not like when my two were small. Enjoy it, won't you? It goes *so* quickly.' She moved on, not expecting an answer, her patent shoes striking the ground purposefully.

Marjorie followed her for a hundred yards or so thinking. Thing is, I had a life that did not quite become.

In the pawn shop the range of goods was astonishing. In old oak cabinets with bevelled glass the unclaimed merchandise was roughly displayed. Under low lights and thick dust lay diamond rings in velour cases, set next to shiny grey plastic gun-shaped hairdryers, trailing knotted wires. There was an elaborate silk tie in a squashed Hermès box, which Hugh would have loathed. Marjorie, with May sleeping in the old blue pram, looked at every single thing, as if there was something very particular she was searching out. The man in there was pleasant enough, he left her alone. As she had nothing to get rid of she pretended to be on the look-out – she wouldn't have him thinking her and May odd. She asked to look at a gold fountain pen, asked if she might see how it wrote. 'What a shame. It's too thick, you see,' she said, when her writing came out chubby and squished.

'Not to worry,' the man said. 'How old?' He smiled.

'Twenty-six,' she said, after a pause.

'Twenty-six weeks?'

'Oh, the baby!'

'I wouldn't ask a lady her age, now, would I?'

'No, of course,' she said, 'I'm s-sorry,' and promptly she shifted round the unwieldy pram and marched out into the street, but the following day she returned and, to justify herself, she bought a clumsy-looking silver-plated mileometer with a clip that attached to a belt or lapel. On a whim she wheeled the pram in a northerly direction for two hours until the little black arrow pointed to the number six. She was somewhere near the North Circular, starving, her afternoon clothes not warm enough for the evening gloom. She pushed the pram into a kosher Chinese restaurant because it had a wide door. It was entirely empty. Possibly it wasn't even open. A Chinese woman brought her cushions and a bowl of soup and a blue-and-white china spoon. She held May, who had woken up, while Marjorie ate quickly. The woman was kind and sang a Chinese nursery rhyme to the baby. Marjorie's soup bowl filled with tears. 'My husband died,' Marjorie whispered, but the woman didn't hear.

'You want to telephone him?' she asked. 'He come pick you up?'

A widow and a mother, those were her jobs now. In the chemist a crisp poster said, 'Make room for some "Me" time in your day and you'll feel more happy and confident.' At school she had dreamed of helping out in a theatrical agency, but that seemed like a different person's lifetime. They took their turns to cry, Marjorie and May, and sometimes they cried together, but it never felt like conversation, just two people talking over each other.

It was unclear for much of the time what it was that had happened. There'd been an accident followed by some sort of eviction from the life she thought she'd had. What she did not understand, what she was reaching for: if things could change so quickly, did it mean she was insubstantial as a person? If her thoughts, feelings, responses, her daily routine could alter so completely in one hour, then had she really had purchase on any of them? Had she not been pieced together properly to begin with? Was there something low-grade about her, her reality or her grasp? And now everything slipped through her fingers. *Don't forget the baby!* she consoled herself. *Hold on to the baby, won't you?* But what was a baby exactly? Sometimes at night it was a little sweet animal in fancy dress, its eyes huge and dark and twitching, with little irregular grunting noises. Sometimes the animal seemed more menacing, a miniature rodent, heaving and sharp-gummed, a floppy, round-girthed creature, who made strange, jerking movements, intense and inhuman with its little nips and its shrieking. Sometimes the eyes appalled. The baby was like a little factory. It was not complicated. You could get the measure of its continual mechanic gear. Change, feed, sleep. Change, feed, sleep. Sometimes it was best not to let it get too personal. The health visitor said the baby was thriving. 'You're doing so well,' she said. That was that.

She returned to the pawn shop most days. When you asked the man who worked there, 'How are you?', he always said exactly the same thing: 'Oh, the usual. Same story. You know the score.' He was solidly built with a boxer's crooked face, which had a permanent tan. Round his neck was a chain of heavy rose-gold links. Once he told her, 'We got a mink coat in yesterday. Beautiful, it is. Italian. Top quality. Trouble is, it's only got one arm! Client said she'll bring the other in today. Believe it when I see it, I said to myself. Still,' he reasoned. 'Still.' He handed May a grubby pink rabbit, and unwrapped a chocolate toffee from a long tube and put it into the baby's hand. Marjorie laughed. It was the day she had decided to give May her first solid food and had spent much of the morning poaching and sieving a small amount of a William's pear. Deftly, she prised the sweet from May's fist and transferred it to her own mouth.

'It's a delicate business, this one. You need tact and under-standing. Nothing shocks me, you see, and that's why I'm cut out for the work. My father was an undertaker. Had premises over Kensal Green way. They always got him to tidy the deceased for the family, make them look nice, make them look their best. People had a lot of open coffins then. They don't so much now. He taught me a lot. It broke his heart that I didn't want to go into the business but I saw the toll it takes. The people who work with the dead have a lot of health problems. They don't look after themselves. I don't know why. It's stressful, I suppose. There's lot of drinking. A lot of comfort eating. I can't explain. He said, my father said, "When there's a deceased person in the room people will say or do anything." It acts like a – well, it frees them up. You'd be amazed what comes out. Sometimes I think it's a bit the same here.' He looked down at the pram. 'Ah, she's dropping off again. She's just like a little peanut, isn't she?'

Marjorie smiled and nodded. She glanced into her bag at the mileometer. She had more walking to do. They headed up to Golders Green and paid ninety pence for admittance into Anna Pavlova's old house. She felt a sense of pride thicken and redden her blood. It was a proper outing. They were a mother and daughter, after all. They looked at some feathery white costumes appliquéd with silver swans. There were headdresses to match, little pointy ostrich confections with sparkling jewels and ribbon ties. May beamed, and suddenly Marjorie knew it was all right because in almost any human situation love could tip the scales.

Marjorie sat in an armchair at the back of the gift kiosk and discreetly fed May under the folds of her coat, stroking her head. She felt so entirely happy she thought she might just die there and then, or start to dance or burst into tears and never stop with the relief of it all. She kissed May's head and said to her, 'I love you, my darling.' Then something odd happened. A man stumbled over, his hand outstretched. He loomed over her chair, his clothes reeking of tobacco and late nights. He smiled, and there was spittle on his whiskers. 'I love pugs,' he said, as if the information were guaranteed to amuse her. 'I'm stupid about them! Name's Roger.' May started to howl. The man nearly jumped out of his skin. 'What you got in there? A hound?'

'Baby,' Marjorie replied smoothly.

'Ah, the young of the species.' He bowed.

Marjorie nodded. 'Good afternoon,' she said.

She had reached a stage in life that generally went with age. She felt this when her husband had died. All the other widows she'd ever heard of were quite old. Before Hugh's funeral, when she peeked into the mirror, she had looked younger than ever, the first traces of lines at the mouth, round the eyes, had gone and in their place a blank, expressionless terrain stared back. She looked like she did not have a character, let alone any experience. Yet there she was.

Occasionally she re-entered, in her mind, her old haunts, such as the waxworks museum. There were a lot of characters in the office. The woman who managed the admin staff, called Mrs Greenferry, had been an actress in her youth. She had played the female lead in an Ealing comedy about a runaway train but it had never been distributed. Mrs Greenferry, Vera, had an odd sort of effusiveness that struck you as welcoming and cheery, until you realised she did it to everyone – it was absolutely, and in no way, personal. Several of the staff had looked in at the funeral. Mrs Greenferry had worn an enormous fringed black hat. Marjorie thanked her awkwardly. She smiled and pressed her hand. 'Thought I'd make an effort, dear,' she said. 'So rarely get the chance.'

Marjorie took a part-time job at the pawn-brokers, with May generally sleeping for three hours each afternoon in her Moses basket in the back room of the shop. Shame and failure were necessarily part of all the transactions and the pay was dire, but it was oddly soothing. She liked the nature of the exchanges she had and, besides, in reality she spent half of her time stroking May's forehead and feeding her and singing her back to sleep and tickling her toes. For this I get paid! she told herself proudly. When people brought in their goods, women in particular, she was at pains to be complimentary and understanding. By way of training Raymond made her a little introductory speech. His voice was low, his lips moist, because he was thinking. 'If people feel they are losing things you need to make them feel that it's something really worth losing. It's like a kindness to them. That they were privileged to have owned the goods in the first place. That you're impressed by the item. I can't explain why but it makes them feel better. It's human nature, I suppose,' he said.

One day as he was unlocking the shop, flinging open the window cages and pinning them back, he said, 'May I ask how your husband passed away?'

'Knocked down by a car. Driver didn't even stop.'

Raymond shook his head from side to side. He said nothing but, moments later, a large, sugary orange mug of tea appeared at her elbow. Marjorie eked it out for as long as she could. She had the feeling it was the first time in his life he had made a cup of tea for a woman.

It was spring now and Marjorie had nude arms. She wanted to tell him something that would make a difference in a kind way, something gracious, something opaque. She tried things out: 'My heart's on a bit of a budget just now,' but that wouldn't do. Ten weeks passed.

One morning a woman came in with a long rope of pearls

in her hands. 'Cocktail pearls,' she called them. She lassoed her neck with them; they went round it three times. 'No occasion to wear them any more,' she explained simply. 'My daughter didn't want them. Said they were ageing.'

'They're beautiful.' Marjorie leaned forward admiringly. She fetched Raymond to suggest a price.

'You can try them if you like,' the woman said, slipping them off.

'Oh, you're kind, but I'm not really meant—'

Raymond appeared, examined the necklace carefully, coiled it back into its velvet-lined box and wrote the lady a receipt.

Just then the door of the shop slammed open. A slight woman, dark with hard eyes, burst into the room – 'showroom', Raymond termed it. She was angry, spoiling for a fight. The lady with the pearls sprang back, putting her hand to her throat.

Raymond nodded, 'Jacqueline,' he said politely.

She stood between Marjorie and the pearl lady. 'Which is it?' she hissed.

'I'm sorry?' Raymond said.

'Are you Marjorie?'

'Yes.'

'Get your things. You don't work here any more.'

A few days later a note arrived at Homer Rise with a cheque covering her wages to the end of the month. 'So sorry, mate. I think I love you. I can't see you again.'

For a while after that Bette came to the house most days in her lunch-hour, mopping them all up a bit, bringing flowers and sandwiches.

'Am I managing, Bette?' Marjorie asked.

'Course you are,' her friend said, but she kept on coming. Sometimes she stroked Marjorie's forehead as she entertained her with gossip from the bank – who was in and who was out – and tales of her own disastrous love-life. She had a puppy now, called Alan. 'Bit of company for me.'

Marjorie felt unsure. She did not say many things because her thoughts were so abstract, funny bits of muddle and clatter. 'How do you get people in your life?' she wanted to ask. 'Is your personality something your body is meant to wear or is it more set?' Finally she did ask a question: 'If you genuinely think about yesterday and you can't remember a single thing, nothing comes through at all, is it a bad sign?'

Bette had settled May into her Moses basket and was taking a sponge cake out of the oven, setting it to cool on a wire rack. 'Oh, listen, everyone wonders about that stuff sometimes. You'll be fine.'

Marjorie peered at her surroundings. Had the room always had so many alcoves? Surely not?

They took short walks, the three of them, with the pram, but it was difficult. Sometimes the street scenes looked so fragile, the pedestrians wafer-thin and all the roads feeding into each other, but what did it amount to? The tulips in the park were falling apart. Could you decide to be small in your life? Not everybody needed a luminous backdrop. Sometimes Hugh sneezing in a really nice way could make you happy for hours. She thought of her father always apologising until he apologised his way right out of their lives for good. Physical things helped. 'I must be going mad, Bette, because yesterday I couldn't stop thinking that I wish I had more muscles.'

'That's not mad. It's just the fashion!' Bette said cheerily.

'We could all go for a swim at the weekend, if you're not doing anything, perhaps?'

'I'd like that.'

'It's a date, then.' Bette spoke so kindly that her words seemed to have a sort of bloom on them.

One day when Bette came Marjorie was counting out pills on the floor. 'I've got seven different kinds in five colours. A hundred and twelve altogether,' Marjorie remarked animatedly. May lay next to her mother on a sheepskin rug.

Bette was furious. It was the only ever time. 'Get them out of my sight!' she screamed.

'Sorry.' They never mentioned it again.

Five

On Thursday night Marjorie met a colleague for a drink. They had done their marriage-guidance training together ten years earlier. 'D'you think I've got what it takes?' Colin had asked her warily, at their first residential training weekend. 'D'you think I'm up to the job? Be brutally honest. I can take it.' His face was quivering, but he had squared up to her, hardening his eyes for the blow.

'But I hardly know you, Colin,' she replied.

'Give me your first impressions, though. Give me your first impressions. Don't hold back.' Colin said he was studying to become a counsellor because his fiancée had recently broken off their engagement. 'She said I crowded her,' he whispered, 'didn't give her enough space, and what I need to know is, is it me or is it her? If you're getting married to someone shouldn't they want to spend time with you? Am I being a fool? Are you good at that kind of thing? You seem very sorted.'

Colin arrived at the pub on his bicycle, which had a skewed back wheel and no lights. He sat down next to her, threw off his waterproof jacket and came straight to the point. He wanted

Marjorie's advice. 'It's all the people I'm seeing. They're nuts. One minute the men are laying into their wives as if they're evil witches and then suddenly they turn round and it's crystal clear to everyone that what they're practically saying is, "You never ever had any time for me when I was a kid." And we sit there, the three of us, wallowing in the horrible mess, and he's deliberately seeking coldness in her to reinforce some childhood discomfort that he has a love-hate relationship with, and she's fed up with copping the whack for his mother's lack of maternal feelings and feeling cooler towards him by the day – i.e., fitting in with his worst fears, or hopes or what-have-you, and I'm sitting there panicking like crazy wishing I had more . . . I don't know . . . Skills, aptitude? I don't know what it is. I can't manage the workload, Marjorie. I'm thinking of taking a year off, go on some courses. Travelling? Do you know what I mean? What d'you think I should do? I've got four weeks of holiday coming up soon. Do you think I'm cracking up? How does anyone manage?'

Marjorie took a breath. 'It does sound a little over-whelming. I wonder . . . Shall I get some drinks or something?' she asked.

'Sorry,' he said. 'Yeah, great. Guinness for me. And a packet of dry roasted, if I may. Actually, make that two packs. I skipped lunch.'

Marjorie returned with the drinks and snacks. 'Have you talked to your supervisor about any of this? Is there a way you could cut back on your workload without letting any-one down?'

But Colin had not quite stopped talking. 'You see, if I had someone myself I don't think all this would get to me in the same way. It wouldn't have to mean so much. D'you know what I mean?'

Marjorie sighed. 'And there's no one you like?'

'It's not so much a question of me liking someone as a question of them, you know, liking me.'

Marjorie nodded. 'Right.'

'Don't mention this to anyone, will you?, but sometimes,' he said, 'when my clients are really going at each other, I find it reassuring. Doesn't make me feel such a loser. D'you think that's bad?'

'Well . . .' Marjorie pondered the question. 'I suppose if that's how you genuinely feel, as long as you fully acknowledge it to yourself to the extent that it doesn't influence the way you conduct yourself with your patients, then I suppose—'

'Sometimes I worry that they might be having a go at each other to please me!'

'Well, I suppose that might be an area that needs care-ful—'

'Fuck it! They all deserve each other, don't they?'

Marjorie's lips were pursed. She glanced up at the clock that ticked loudly above the ugly square mahogany bar and saw that since Colin's arrival on his bicycle only seventeen minutes had elapsed.

'I've been going to a few talks at the Institute. See if I can get some new ideas. Those psychoanalysts are a crazy bunch,' Colin continued. 'Yesterday, right, I went to this meeting and there were six speakers. From all over the world. One from the Ukraine, even. And d'you know what the subject was? Go on, have a guess.'

'Oh, no,' Marjorie said. 'I'm terrible at guesses.'

'No, have a crack at it. You'll never guess in a million years.'

'Dreams?' Marjorie offered flatly.

'No way! Listen to this, what they were squabbling about, these six international guys with their poncy attaché cases and their slick suits and their what-have-you, what was really tearing them apart was – listen to this – was whether there should be a hyphen between "psycho" and "analysis".'

'No!' Marjorie said limply.

There were not two but countless factions, he informed her. She might not understand it but to some the word 'psychoanalyst' represented a trademark, recognition of this set of practitioners as the premium brand, linked to a small number of training centres, the acknowledged world leaders, the Rolls-Royces of the therapeutic world, if you like. As a concession, one idea mooted was that splinter groups from newer, less copper-bottomed training centres might be allowed to call themselves psycho-analysts with a hyphen, and that the next rung down on the ladder from still well-respected but not top-drawer institutes could be called psychoanalysts*, with no hyphen but with the addition of an asterisk. He shrugged his shoulders. 'Fascinating stuff, don't you think?'

'Will the next step down be inverted commas?' Marjorie asked.

Colin laughed. 'Nice one,' he said. 'Those wise guys are full of surprises. Watch this space.'

It was shortly after May's eighth birthday that Marjorie started having strong feelings that things were not as they should be, dim fears that she was not good with people or with anything, really, cats, cars. There were simple things about the workings of men and women and children that she failed to grasp. How did you know those things? How did anyone? And these were just the most rudimentary aspects. As for anything more advanced . . . why, she was utterly in the dark. She was certain her mother had not known, but that was hardly an excuse. Marjorie had the sense that she was falling into bad habits. That she was failing. Nothing serious. Small things. Only sometimes when May was at school she felt so sad she could barely operate herself. And yet when May emerged for their after-school celebratory reunions Marjorie felt things were not going so well there either: May lagged a couple of paces behind her, vague and uncertain, as they made their habitual rounds of cafés and toy shops, with their animal noises and their cuddling. Was there something shrill about the proceedings now? Something forced? Something crazy? Marjorie longed for the early days when May had been so happy to see her it was practically amorous.

Sometimes May had a friend over and Marjorie could not think of a single thing to do or say. They had their routines, mother and daughter, their regular private festivities, but the presence of another person altered everything. Marjorie felt her heart seep out of her and they would stand there in the doorway, the three of them, staring at their shoes, the little girls' hands fiddling expectantly. What did they want from her? How could she show them they were welcome to the best she had? Were they safe? She tried to get inspiration for conversations from radio plays she heard while ironing in the afternoons. She noted down the dialogue neatly: 'Would you like a drink? Are you hungry? Did your mother knit that scarf for you? What do you like doing in your spare time?' But when she put these questions they seemed the wrongest possible things. Would they guess she was trying to express her care? Some strange notions came to light around this time. For instance, one day she felt so angry with Hugh's chairs for clogging up all the space in the house that she hurled one across the room. She hoped she had not lost her sense of humour. But even still. She wondered about her idea of training to be a teacher. Would it be as bad but on a vaster scale? Then, one evening, Marjorie heard a programme on the radio and the woman talking said one side-effect of training to become a marriage counsellor was that *all* her real-life relationships had improved beyond her wildest dreams. Marjorie sat up. She noted down the number.

The panel who interviewed her for the counselling diploma told her gently that they thought she was suffering from depression. She thanked them warmly. She was over the moon. 'I just *knew* it was something,' she said. They told her to get some help with it, come back in a year and they would reconsider her application. Next year they had listened intently when she had talked about the intricacies of the relationships between men and women in the plays and novels she had been studying, and then they had said it: 'You're in!' Afterwards – three miracles. The course was more interesting than anything she had ever seen or done before. She adored it. She came first in her year.

Helen Braintree was in high spirits as she flounced into Marjorie's consulting room and spread out in her chair. 'You see, he still hasn't said it. He's got until six today to apologise or I'm out. I made it quite clear.'

'Yes,' Mark confirmed it drily, 'the clock is most certainly ticking. I think she's hoping for a last-minute settlement on the steps of the court, as it were, suitcase in hand.'

'I am glad you're finding it all so amusing.'

'Well, you should listen to yourself sometimes. I'm sure the humour of the situation wouldn't escape even you.'

'So I'm humourless as well now, am I?'

'Well, you know it's not your strong point.'

'And it's yours?'

'It isn't a competition.'

'It isn't? How did I manage to get that so wrong?'

'It seems to come quite naturally with you.'

'It must be exhausting to be so right all the time.'

'Well, it certainly takes its toll.'

'No wonder you look so haggard.'

'Sweet, isn't she?'

Marjorie peered closely at the Braintrees, taking in all the steps of the little entertainment they were staging for her sake. There was no doubt that they were enjoying themselves, with their sophisticated Punch and Judy routine. Helen's cheeks had the hint of rose glow and Mark was positively blooming, excited little spots of saliva moistening the corners of his lips. He stretched out in his chair in a way that reminded both women of how much he admired his legs.

Helen glanced at her watch. 'You may like to know that you have seventy-two minutes remaining.'

'Do remind me to savour your presence for every one of them, won't you? Shouldn't we really be spending them alone?'

Somehow, when they were conducting themselves in this

jauntily combative manner, they seemed to find each other particularly appealing. Meanwhile, embarrassment was ripening on Marjorie's face. She felt its anxious warmth spreading in her armpits. Her toes curled in their ladylike shoes, which, when she looked at them, struck her as faintly ridiculous, as ridiculous as the Braintrees with their heartless pantomime.

It was a fear she regularly nursed that her ultra-feminine person – the creamy skin, the luscious yet controlled arrangement of flesh, which came in for its fair share of admiration – was not so much feminine as ladylike: that is, an approximation or imitation or even a parody of femininity, rather than the thing itself. At worst, she could see, she might be taken for effeminate.

'Darling, how much time do I have now?'

'You have sixty minutes,' Helen said dully. 'An hour.'

'And you genuinely promise to move out in under an hour?' Mark's face was all keen anticipation. 'Do you swear to it?'

Marjorie decided to take things in hand. 'I don't want to speak out of turn but it seems to me that treating this issue like a game isn't really working for either of you. I think it's a gamble you don't really want to take. You don't seem to see that you're playing with fire.' Yet she did not say these things: they did not strike the right note. They were both too personal (too personal to Marjorie) and at the same time confusingly unspecific. She tried a different tack: 'Mark, you may remember a week or two ago you and I spoke alone while Helen was out of the room. Would you mind if I drew on some of our conversation from then?'

Mark made a courteous open-handed gesture as if she were

an ungainly pedestrian he might allow speedily to cross in front of his awfully grand motor-car. 'Be my guest.'

'You said to me, I think, that one of the reasons you avoided making apologies was because you thought that with them might come responsibilities. Have you thought about that any more?'

'I have, actually.'

'What you said to me on that day, or what we seemed to agree on, was that part of your difficulty about apologising came from a sense that nothing you could do really had the power to affect another person.'

'What I was thinking was this: the trouble with Helen and me is that in a lot of ways our similarities are what drew us together but they're also exactly what we loathe in each other. I think that possibly the only things we have in common are our bad qualities.

'Of course, they're worse in me but, then, that's just natural vanity on my part. Not that she doesn't have her share of that, but it illustrates exactly what I was saying. I admit I have my heartless side, and it's not something I'm very proud of, but who doesn't?' Mark spoke calmly with a degree of mirth. 'That's why I don't think we should have a baby. I'm sure it would be a vile little beast.'

And then, suddenly, it wasn't funny any more. The atmosphere altered dramatically. When Marjorie turned to Helen it was straight away apparent that she was trying not to cry, but almost immediately heaving dry sobs were rising up and up in her and then she broke and her head shook and the tears came coursing down her cheeks and she turned her shoulders in and her whole body shrank into itself and its deepening despair.

She sat there howling, half choking as she tried to catch her breath between sobs. Then she raised her head, her mouth a contorted hoop of pain. Her face drenched with tears, her running nose, her eyes stung raw and red at him, by him, by her own attempts to temper her rage. Mark was turned away from her and, with her hands outstretched, she made a kind of anguished plea. 'You . . .' she spluttered. 'You . . . you just hurt me *so much*. I can't – I just can't bear it.' Her small frame was heaving jaggedly; her arms, which were huddled tightly around her chest, clasped her shoulders.

In an instant Mark was out of his chair and at her side. 'Helen,' he said stiffly. He took one of her hands and kissed it, then folded behind her ear some loose strands of hair that were covering her eye. 'I'm so sorry.' His voice had dropped gently for sincerity. Marjorie held her breath. And in an instant it came over his face that he *was* hugely sorry, and also sad and lonely and ashamed. 'I love you.'

'Well, help me, then,' Helen said. 'I need your help . . .'

God, I'm good, Marjorie thought, as she fed her arms through the sleeves of her coat and removed a piece of thread from her lapel. She was experienced enough to know it was always three steps forward two steps back, but it was a start. She wandered down the corridor of the Centre in celebratory mode. She glanced around to make sure no one was looking, and then introduced a couple of skips into her gait and one of those sideways jumps where you click your heels in the air, something at which Hugh had excelled.

Elated, Marjorie proceeded directly to the staffroom and its kettle. She wondered if her daughter was in. There's a lot to be said for trial and error, she thought vaguely. Much more than people think. Her colleague, David Phillips, was picking up dirty cups, peering at them to see which was the least unhygienic. Since his wife had left, his appearance had suffered terribly. It was not just a matter of laundry and pressing, although such processes had evidently ceased abruptly: something in his face had collapsed so that, despite his otherwise slender frame, all the blustery softness of his visage had slid downwards. The skin on his forehead looked thin and parched, there was something papery about his eye sockets, but his nose and cheeks and chin were larded with all this extra pink flesh, giving him the appearance of a tragic-looking dog. What had caused this change? Marjorie wondered. Heartbreak? Drink?

Marjorie washed two cups and handed him one. 'Milk and two sugars, isn't it?' Possibly he hadn't eaten in some days. 'I've got a sausage roll in my bag – you can have it, if you like. It's today's.'

'No, thanks.' He shook his head forlornly. 'Apparently I'm flaky enough.'

'That's nonsense.' There was something about his general state of collapse that made Marjorie spry and prim. 'Now, then. You're one of the most conscientious people I know.'

'D'you think?'

It was not exactly the truth but 'Of course. Goodness me.'

'Can I ask you something?'

'What's that?'

'How do people, you know . . . how do people of our age . . . how do they meet people?'

'Oh.' Marjorie took a step back. 'All sorts of ways. All *sorts* of ways.'

'Such as?'

'There's the obvious, of course, pubs and clubs and parties, supermarkets, through friends, at church. Of course, an awful lot of people advertise.'

'Yes, an awful lot of awful people.'

'Not at all. That might once have been the case but nowadays it's perfectly respectable, especially if you choose the right . . . organ.' She hurried on: 'I've heard of literally millions of couples—'

'Really?'

'Of course!'

'Not that I'm fussy.' He shrugged. 'How did you meet your husband? Tilly and I met on a train. I'd never known anything like it.'

'Yes, trains can be . . . good.'

'It was one of those things where in half an hour your whole life changes. She was straight away the nicest person I'd ever met. Serene, discreet. Highly attractive, you know, in the quietest way. She was escorting her nephew back from Oxford, a four-year-old, and the way she treated him – the snacks she had prepared, the brilliant games and the books. She was so full of praise and admiration. Everything she said seemed designed to bolster him up, make him feel appreciated, but it wasn't embarrassing or deliberate or anything. Utterly natural. The boy adored her. Still does. Nice fellow. His own mother hasn't much time for him. She's completely wrapped up in herself. You know, it was one of the most pleasurable journeys I've ever had, just sitting opposite them for an hour.

I remember at one point he wet his trousers and she was marvellous about it. No cross words, she turned the whole thing into a game and had a change of clothes for him there and then, and a towel and everything, and she did it all so gently and discreetly and with so much respect for his, well, for his dignity. As though it were the easiest thing in the world.'

Marjorie poured boiling water into two cups and prodded the teabags with the back of a spoon.

'I do think it's important to respect the dignity of children,' he said dreamily.

'I quite agree. I think it's a matter of human rights.' She handed him the tea.

'I've got this couple coming this afternoon and he's a bit grumpy and she's a bit of a nag but basically they're nice people, funny and tender, and I feel like saying to them, "What the hell are you doing here? You don't know how lucky you are." And, you know, they've no idea at all. They think they're so miserable and he's half an hour late once a week and she buys too many dresses for their girls, and that's about as rough as it gets. It beggars belief. I feel like saying to them, "People would kill for what you've got." D'you ever feel like that?'

'It does sound a strange situation. I suppose there's always the possibility that there's something big they haven't yet been able to tell you.'

'Well, here's hoping!' He opened the door with his back and his elbow clutching his tea tightly to his chest, his sauce-stained jacket flapping cheerily behind him. 'By the way,' he called back. 'Like the dress. It really suits you.'

She had barely admitted it to herself but, of late, her clothes had been not a little inspired by Rose Dempsey's crisp and nursy style. She had found herself leaning towards garments with a slight flavour of the uniform, shirt-waisters seemed to have a new appeal, collars and cuffs had become a bit of a feature and, on one occasion, button-down epaulettes had made an appearance. How could it hurt?

It would have been so easy for Hugh not to have come into her life. Their meeting – which had been random in the extreme, she often felt – made more sense in light of the fact that two and a half years after that first encounter she and May were shovelling earth.

Marjorie had only slipped through the wide oak doors into the church hall on account of the thick sheet of hail that, out of the blue, had thrashed against her face, stinging and soaking her so violently that, despite her waterproofed blue overcoat and her cardigan and her vest and tights and woollen skirt – with its sharp inverted pleat – even the thin scalloped waistband of her knickers was wet. But hadn't she landed on her feet?

A bearded man of middle height stood at the front of the room, addressing his audience in mature, considered tones. It was a narrow hall, Victorian, dusty, cream-painted, with a stage at the far end shielded by rust-coloured velvet drapes. Next to the speaker a wall-mounted blackboard bore, in white upper-case letters, the words 'PERSONALITY AND ITS DISCONTENTS', the last letter dangling wildly like a hook. Forty men and women sat in rows in front of the speaker, some scratching away at notebooks. All wore concentrated expressions on their faces, their jerseys brown and shades of unripe green. Marjorie lurked at the back of the room, pressing her damp body into the burning folds of the radiator. Smells of wool and scorch rose up and she breathed in deeply, relaxing into her new surroundings, dabbing at her face, which was freckled with wet, and fiddling absently with her hair.

The man was talking grandly about stick insects: their triumphs, their failures. He referred to some notes in a scientific-looking journal. The previous year, he related, a group of behavioural scientists from London University went to a part of northern Brazil that had a high population of stick insects and studied an area of about a hundred metres square. They identified all the birds and animals that were the natural predators of larger insects in this region, then systematically examined the guts of a controlled sample of the creatures to see what, exactly, they were eating. To the astonishment of all concerned, and despite their obvious efforts at body camouflage, stick insects were extremely well represented in the insides of these animals. Although they had adapted and evolved, limiting and reducing their form and antics to avoid a certain fate, it had all been in vain. That hanging about pretending to be sticks had fooled not a soul. The disguise, the severe restrictions, the pretence – futile. They had wholly underestimated their predators. So much for their cunning. So much for their know-how. Did they think the rest of the world had been born yesterday?

The lecturer took a droll little step back, inclined his head and regarded his audience, like a comedian who had just delivered a punchline and was waiting for it to take.

His intelligent, humorous glance indicated that he would not be so crass as to extrapolate out of this example of evolutionary wrongheadedness something belonging to a more obviously human domain, but his bent head, his sharp, watery eyes, his quivering top lip – well, you could see he was tempted.

Curt smiles of recognition flickered through the audience. A man raised his arm to fire a question and Marjorie saw, in his outstretched hand, the programme for the talk, which had London Psychoanalytical Society printed on its cover. She must be in a hall full of psychoanalysts! She made a slow circle of the room with her eyes. She did not know whether to laugh or to cry. New in London, installed in a small bed-sitter in a basement near Baker Street, she was so lonely for company that some nights she used to wander across Marylebone station with the dim hope she might be bumped into by someone who was not too busy or cross.

Presently there was a lull in the questions. Through the high, arched windows of the still hall Marjorie saw that the rain had stopped and she slipped out again into the street on to the pavement, which glowed black with rainfall and small, soft, dark deposits of ice, and she was so absorbed by this notion of risk and gain and birds' intestinal tracts and the intelligent, spry noses of the specialist congregation that she did not notice another member of the audience who had slipped out with her, and then, when she had turned back on herself swiftly, in the direction of the waxworks museum, not looking where she was going, CRASH, she had collided with a man. It was quite hard: there were bumps and bruises. But how impressive he'd been as they untangled themselves: his limbs, long and spry, were somehow quite specifically entwined with hers at the elbow joints, at the backs of their knees, at the wrists. It had taken some undoing, their separation. She felt his breath on her fingers, his shoes by her ribs. For a moment they were Siamese twins. Marjorie pulled sharply at her skirt, making herself decent, sending automatic hand to untamed hair. Might he have seen a flash of her second-worst underwear? It didn't bear thinking. Hugh was hugely apologetic, but elegantly so, and gracious and easy and concerned. Then, to her complete surprise, introductions came and even coy handshakes, when moments earlier they had been as good as on top of each other. Afterwards Hugh asked if she'd care for a cup of tea at his shop.

'Your shop?' She could not quite work it out.

'I've got a shop round the corner,' he explained. 'I close for lunch. I like doing different things with the time. I ought to stay open but—'

'Oh, no, I mean, you've got to live your life, haven't you?' Her voice was skittish, almost hysterical. How could she be so bold?

She had not agreed to the tea but she could not help noticing she was following him down the high street, almost jogging to keep up. The pavement was streaked with wet beneath her feet and she slipped about in her shoes, which were too big and felt like little boats. All her senses were dangerously alive. She caught the reek of fried lunches, pies, and grilled or melted cheese from corner pubs, her brain straining to record the broken ends of songs that blared out into the streets. She regarded her new companion closely in her mind's eye where the thin May breeze tickled the dark mop of curls on his head. His eyes were green lights and looked no strangers to mirth, and his large hands and the pale skin on his neck looked luxuriously smooth. His nose was big, almost remarkably so, with a strong presence and whole features of its own, such as a transparent pockmark at the bridge and a sharp pink line on the right side near the nostril but, on the whole, it was a nose to be admired. Without it, he wouldn't have been half the man he was, Marjorie judged.

'Not long to go now.'

'What?'

'We're almost there.'

She imagined a gentlemen's outfitter's crammed with rolls of brownish tweed and bolts of striped cotton shirting. No, that was not right. She could not picture him with a tape-measure slung round his neck, the little black printed increments like insects, the cool brass ends flapping at his wrists. It was both too grave and too frivolous for him. Inside legs – for goodness' sake!

She situated him in a small, grey-painted gallery hung with gilt-framed landscapes, greenish and orangy, talking knowledgeably with a customer, a client, about light-fall. That wasn't it either. It wouldn't be something so dry. She decided to ask him.

'I sell chairs,' he said. 'Old ones. It was my father's shop. Hemming and Son. I'm the son. He asked me to carry it on so I did. Get one or two nice things now and then.'

'I love chairs,' Marjorie did not quite say. Instead: 'Does it get much passing trade or . . . not really?'

'Oh, no. It's in a rather odd area with lots of other funny shops nobody much visits. But I do all right.'

'Oh, I didn't mean—'

'Got a couple of new ones in this morning. I'll show you, if you like. They're quite good, I think.'

He stopped in front of a large, grand-looking antiques shop. 'This is me,' he said. *Hemming and Son* was written in gold on black above the window. A sharp bell sounded as they walked into the showroom. Marjorie stepped carefully across the elderly-looking carpet, which was neither quite green nor grey. There must have been eighty chairs in the room, which was really two shops knocked together, three times as wide as it was deep. The walls were painted a watery brown colour. In the air there was a dim scent of turpentine.

Just then the afternoon gloom was punctuated by a sudden flash of sunshine, which streamed into the shop and made snowflake patterns on Marjorie's shoes. 'Take a seat!' Hugh smiled. It felt like the most generous offer in the world. 'These are the new ones I mentioned. What d'you think?' He gestured towards two large gold-framed French armchairs covered in threadbare raspberry *toile de Jouy*. 'They're surprisingly comfy,' he said.

Marjorie sat down with extreme caution. What are you doing here? she asked herself, sensing her own foolishness ripening on her cheeks. Even the backs of her knees felt flushed.

'Won't be a moment.' Hugh disappeared and returned soon after holding a tray with three cups on it and a jug of milk. 'I didn't know if you preferred tea or coffee,' he said, 'so I made both.'

Marjorie told him that, since leaving college five weeks ago, she had started work at the London Waxworks Museum, on the second floor (Monarchy, History, Showbiz) for most of the time, but twice already she had been allowed to help out in the workshops, which was what she really liked. Now and then, she confided, she had done a bit of modelling for the sculptors who worked away in the building's vaults. 'If you looked carefully at the back of Mary Queen of Scots's head you might just recognise something of me, one of these days,' she remarked casually, 'not that I think I'm – you know. I mean, they get all the girls to do it. I do the odd stint in the gift shop too. I have to wear a uniform . . . Oh, black and white . . . It doesn't do a lot for me. It's a temporary thing. I know it's time to get a proper job, really. I'm not getting any younger.' She was twenty-three. 'I'm keeping an eye out for something more – more concrete.'

Hugh told her he had dealt in chairs for eleven years. That his father and his grandfather had done so before him. They had built up quite a clientele. Several times he referred to 'my regulars', once with a more serious note of responsibility in his voice, once neutrally and once with a sort of fond exasperation. 'What are they like?' Marjorie wanted to ask, and 'Do you, well – do you kind of love them?'

For a fleeting moment she half envied that he had these people he could call his own, and also that they had him. She surveyed the ranks of chairs, a set of twelve upholstered dining chairs in mahogany and faded apple green leather, with two armed carvers, a pair of ancient-looking red brocade *thrones* (were they?) with gold tassels and sagging quilted oblong roof-type arrangements. Some low-slung nursing chairs, a red morocco sofa so deep and wide that six people could have lain down on it side by side. And what did she have? Random tourists gazing blearily, through the viewfinders of cameras, at rows and rows of fake people (they weren't even made of wax any more but a modern substitute, which was part fibreglass and part plastic), before eagerly snapping up postcards and camera film and celebrity statuettes. Colleagues who – it seemed – would rather be mauled by sharks than speak a civil word to her, let alone invite her round the corner for Coke or currant buns or whatever it was they did in their small chattering packs without her. The exhibits themselves: cold, ghostly models of the rich and famous, expertly fashioned and dressed by a team of serious professionals and arranged – arrayed – in random settings, royal drawing rooms, battle scenes, torture chambers, red-carpet premières like so many half-crazed, rootless outpatients. Only a lunatic would say it was the same.

Hugh was excessively interested in everything she said – physically so, you could see it in his eyes, in his ears, even, his tensed, round shoulders. An amazing listener, alert and good-natured, he made all the words you used feel like they had never been used before. And because of this she started speaking quite wildly. She liked the theatrical note that had crept into her voice. It seemed festive, celebratory. Normally she kept her cards close to her chest, but this afternoon she scarcely recognised herself. Her sister, she explained, was discomforted by 'even the most basic tenets of modern life', and instead of trying to fit herself to live in the world was always trying to get the world to budge so that it more closely resembled how she saw it. What a great idea that was not! The head of the museum, Mrs Lorraine Geddes, well, it was said by some that she had only made a career in wax because anyone else she quite literally bored to tears. Marjorie rambled on aimlessly, losing sight of herself in the luxury of his rapt attention – and how it had delighted him. In thirty-nine days at the museum no one had spoken to her an unnecessary word. She did not wish to bend his ears overly, but she *was* starving. She was quite used to lingering in shops so that remarks might be addressed to her. She looked on every bus-ride as an opportunity for society. If you booked an alarm call through the operator for the following day, she discovered, when you finished the transaction the operator generally said, 'Good night,' with some sweetness, but when the bill came she was horrified: these specialist calls with the personal touch cost £2.25 a throw. She was new to London. Hugh had lived here all his life. She felt like the greenest possible fool.

Hugh did not say a great deal, but when he did speak it was with kindness and ease. In no way did he find her irksome. That was what she could not have borne. He dropped one or two comments about the talk they had attended. At one point, as an aside, he said something along the lines of 'Everything that's to do with people is of huge interest to me.' She'd never heard anything like it. It seemed he really stood for things. All human experience he considered highly valuable. 'Have you never met someone you didn't admire?' Marjorie almost asked, but she let it go for it struck her suddenly that, as a line of enquiry, it was cheap. She could not have him think her a lightweight.

She knew she had her peculiarities, her bizarre little likes and dislikes, but Hugh's qualities were real, things that would reckon up high scores against universal, world-class standards, she could not help feeling.

Towards the end, with teaspoons and empty cups sitting on the tray between them – she had drunk the tea and then the coffee – Marjorie let slip the piece of information that was, to her, the most important fact of her life. Two years earlier her mother had died. She was always on Marjorie's mind now: Marjorie's happiness, like a child's, was still firmly in her mother's hands. Very occasionally a couple of hours went by when her mother was lost to her thoughts, but that was just a different kind of agony. Marjorie spoke openly about this subject. She wanted her grief to sound not unserious but, somehow, with a lightness and movement to it. Sometimes the thoughts were more like darting pictures that came to her, flickering, colourful, intense: out of the blue she would see the taut, curious curve of her mother's mouth as she peered at herself uncertainly in the oval hall mirror, or her mother standing at the stove stirring and smiling, a domestic postcard from the past. After eighteen months or so people had said that within two years things changed, and now they said, just as surely as they had put it to her before, 'Oh, it takes three or four years. Minimum. You need to allow at least that.'

'It takes as long as it takes,' she murmured, into the air, as if she'd been alone.

'It takes as long as it takes,' Hugh echoed.

As she spoke Marjorie felt a loose tear welling on the underside of her eye but when it came up she just swatted it away. To have harnessed it towards some kind of appeal to a – to a man, of all people, would have been a disgrace, although it would have been a lie to say she had not already wondered if the quality of her grief might impress him. A poem by Tennyson she liked was called deeply religious because of the quality of its doubt. Might not loss say the same about love?

'She'd have really liked you,' Marjorie did not say. 'Oh, yes,' she did not add, not nodding sagely or underwriting the statement with 'Believe you me', as she wanted to, like someone in a play, although it was a phrase she had never uttered in her life. Her mother had not really gone in for liking people, if the truth be known, and wasn't it odd how this had made the loss of her so much more unbearable? Yet Marjorie needed to state something. How else could she convey the sharply overwhelming sensations she found herself feeling without marking herself out as a crazy? She thought about it a little more. And then she struck out for herself boldly. She struck out for – well, for them. She felt her forearm extend fully from the elbow joint, towards him, the whole flirtatious span of it. She faced him open-handed. 'I really, really love your shop,' was what came out. 'I think it's marvellous.'

What if, that day, there had been no hail? What if she'd had with her an umbrella? (But she didn't believe in them. 'Take it from me, they certainly do exist,' Hugh said.) What if she'd darted into the smoky, cramped interior of the fish and chicken bar instead of the church hall, or merely wolfed a sandwich in the staffroom at the museum? Marjorie asked herself these questions with serious relish. Could something as random as rainfall or the sad old lot of a stick insect really seal your fate? And suddenly, exactly eight months later (it was a pretty crazy notion), there was going to be a wedding. A wedding at which he would be groom and she would be bride. Her. Of all people!

Six

Marjorie was approaching the end of a session with a couple she had been seeing for two months. They were not hostile to each other exactly, 'It's nothing like that, it's just that we don't seem to have what you would call conversations,' the lady said. Outside her office window the day was flooded with harsh light that made the leaves on the trees look frail. Marjorie heard her voice beginning to speak, her intonation flattish, commonsensical, good-humoured, no more than mildly authoritative but with some occasional notes creeping in that were almost, well, avuncular. 'I have a suggestion to make. It's a talking and listening exercise, really, that many people find quite helpful. You would pick a time every evening, and during that time I'd like one of you to talk uninterrupted for, I don't know, thirty minutes about anything you like: work concerns, funny things you've seen in the street, dreams for the future, anxieties, whatever you like, except things to do solely with your relationship. Meanwhile the other person listens attentively, but doesn't say anything. That's very important. Then, after half an hour, you switch over. I'd like you to try it every day for a week.'

And then, a few minutes later, 'When you say to him, "I just want you to adore me for ever", can you say what you would like him to do that would make you feel that way? Be quite specific, if you can, when you tell him, so that he knows what would . . . do the trick.'

'Well, it would be great if he could put the rubbish out when he gets home sometimes, and if we could meet up for a sandwich at the café next to his office at lunchtime now and then, maybe once a week, and I'd love it if he brought home a bunch of flowers at the weekend, and when I tell him that supper's ready if he could come straight away and not make me call him several times. Shall I go on?'

'You know, that's probably enough to begin with. What do you think, Peter, about what Juliet is asking for?'

'No problemo. Consider it done. But can you tell her to stop slagging off my mum twenty-four seven?'

'Bastard.'

Marjorie took a a deep breath and, very carefully, brought the edges of her palms together. 'It's time now,' she said neutrally. They left, and Marjorie rose grimly and tied the belt of her aubergine wool bouclé coat in a double knot. She began the walk home, slightly claustrophobic and breathless in her over-warm outerwear. She approached the street with the specialist shops and peered carefully into each one. You had to have a certain degree of confidence – or was it vanity? – to back one line of merchandise in this way. Specialisation was one thing, but there was such a thing as biting off your nose to spite your face. Everything was gambling, when you thought about it. Educated guessing. Risk assessment. And yet it was good to have faith, wasn't it? To come out for what you believed in. Wasn't it?

She saw that a new little boutique called Sew Be It had opened; it sold buttons and buckles, and a small selection of ribbon and millinery accessories, embroidery silks, cotton reels, fancy trimmings and bolts of elaborate braid. But the real boast of the shop was that in a small see-through booth at the front of the store sat a maternal-looking woman with a broad face and a comforting manner who, for £3.25, would match and replace a button for you while you waited. Marjorie lingered by the cash till, her fingers sorting absently through a box of smooth, cool mother-of-pearl buttons, watching the woman at work. Her sewing was dramatic, all the gestures larger than life like a woman sewing symbolically on stage in a ballet or an opera. She made great swooping loops with her needle and thread, pulling the cotton taut with an exaggerated tug, snapping it off with some gleaming embroidery scissors, which were attached by a ribbon to her belt. She wore glasses and approached each commission as though it were a highly skilled activity. 'I can't make it look easy,' she confided to Marjorie, 'not at these prices. They asked me to wear a costume, you know, with a bonnet and everything. I said, "Do I look like a fool?"'

'It is a bit dear, I suppose, but then . . .' She did not wish to be impolite.

'The management is hoping to open a chain of Sew Be Its all over town. They've done a heap of market research. It's going to be the new manicures. It seems men hate sewing on buttons. It's not exactly that they think it's difficult but they're afraid of it, it's all a bit of a mystery, and they don't want to try and fail. They don't want to be found guilty of doing it badly, and the research showed that women don't really think it's acceptable to be asked to sew their men's buttons on, and they say they'll do it but somehow they don't quite get round to it because they mind a little bit, and while all this negotiation goes on or doesn't – well, the button doesn't sew itself and sometimes,' here she lowered her voice to a stage whisper, 'the shirts get thrown away.'

'No!'

'It's true.'

'And the women just don't want to do it?'

'No. Well, mothers do it happily for their children, apparently, but not wives or girlfriends. It's almost impossible to believe, isn't it? I mean if I had . . .' She trailed off.

'Well, quite!' The women's sighs were not without cheer.

'Of course, some of our customers seem to find coming here quite therapeutic. Like pampering. They take me for a bit of an oracle. I suppose I'm what's called a captive audience. They like to ask my advice about things.'

'What sort of things?'

'Oh, you know. Life and so on. From the feminine angle.'

Marjorie smiled and nodded. She tugged at the ribbed lower portion of her fawn-coloured jersey. 'I suppose everyone wants to know about that.'

The women laughed.

'See you, then,' Marjorie said, clutching a tiny wax-paper envelope of shirt buttons. 'And thanks.'

When Marjorie returned to her house the telephone was

ringing. It was May. 'What a lovely surprise.' Marjorie beamed, telephone in one hand, the other disentangling itself from a heavy sleeve, body wriggling free of buttons and knots and belts, but suddenly she froze. She could have kicked herself. She should have avoided the word 'surprise'. She prayed that May would not pick her up on it. She genuinely had not intended any reproach, had she? Had she?

But May was chatting on blithely: 'Just ringing to say I loved your piece in the evening paper last night.'

'My what?'

'Didn't you see it?'

'I don't know what you're talking about. Hang on a moment. I might have it next door. Don't think I threw it away.'

'It's pages twenty-two and twenty-three. Read it, then call me back.' May hung up.

Marjorie rummaged through the pages. And there it was, a huge picture of Rose Dempsey, crisp uniform with the three top buttons undone and a tiny patch of black lace bra peeping through. Her head tilted slightly for emphasis, hands placed firmly on hips, the whole portrait crackled with good sense and high spirits. The accompanying headline said 'TV's Nurse Dempsey's Top Ten Tips'. The premise for the article was that autumn heralded seasonal affective disorder for millions of sufferers nationwide and that Rose Dempsey had some good ideas for combating it. Marjorie sat down to read.

1. Eat a hearty bowl of soup for at least one meal a day – it's healthy, cheery and filling.
2. Always have a small bunch of white freesias on your

bedside table. Even four or five stems in a toothmug will make a difference to your waking mood.

3. Be kind to a stranger today: take cookies to a new neighbour or listen attentively to the person regaling you with their life story on the Underground. You may just learn something.

4. Give 2.5 per cent of your disposable income to charity. ALL MUSLIMS DO. You won't miss it, and it will make you feel good. Plus if everyone did it there'd be no hunger or starvation in the world.

5. You may not have the luxury of half an hour to yourself every day but be sure to take at least three seconds five times a day to check in with yourself. It only takes a moment to say, 'Hi there. You OK?'

6. Once a week have a ridiculously early night and SLEEP for at least nine hours.

7. At least twice a year buy yourself a pair of shoes you feel fabulous in.

8. Once a month clear out a drawer or a cupboard in your home that is full of junk. It will do wonders for your self-esteem. Give away everything that you don't need or love.

9. Once a week devote a day to the person in your life you like most. Give them your undivided attention. Decide they can do no wrong. Let them know how much they mean to you by making no demands or criticisms. Just enjoy the privilege of having that person in your life. Even if it's yourself. Especially if it's yourself.

10. Honour your parents. Take them out for a treat or invite them to join in a regular activity that you enjoy.

They may not be perfect but they won't live for ever and
it will be too late when they're gone.
Above all ENJOY and SHARE.
Rose.
xxxxxx

Marjorie dialled May's number. 'What d'you think?'

'I liked it.'

'So did I. Very much. Thank you for telling me. I must say
she's sensible in a way that's very moving. Stimulating. And
that's unusual. I get the feeling that whatever happened she'd
somehow make it turn out for the best. I've always thought
there was a certain kind of glamour that had a real moral
element to it and I think that's what she's got. A moral
intelligence and yet it never seems dull or conventional.
She makes it seem, well . . . daring. She's such a find, don't
you think?'

May laughed. There was a brief silence. 'I wanted to ask
you something, Mum.'

'Of course you can move back in, May, anytime you like,
just say the word,' Marjorie did not say.

'Yes?'

'If someone wanted to start maybe having marriage guidance
counselling what do they have to do? I mean is there a number
to ring or do they need a note from a doctor or . . . ?

'Well, yes, they can phone direct or they can get a referral
from a GP.'

'It's just a friend and I said I'd ask.'

'Why don't you find a pen while I get the number?'

'Oh, thanks.'

'Not at all. If they want to speak to me or anything, if they've got any queries, do say.'

'I don't think they're quite ready, but—'

'Whatever you think.'

'You'll never guess the latest in our ridiculous little saga,' Mark Braintree's voice was both flat and arch.

'Why d'you have to put it like that? You just love ruining things, don't you?'

'Well, I admit it's always had an appeal.'

'You know, when he was a child he used to spend all his time murdering ants.'

'I invented a sort of guillotine. From modelling clay. It was ingenious. A classic of modern design. If I'd put it into production I could have made a fortune. A killing!'

'What can we do with him?' Helen raised her eyes to the heavens.

'Perhaps you'd like to tell Mrs Hemming the latest in your long line of outrageous requests.'

'Oh shut up! Please. Before we all die of boredom.'

'She only wants a baby. After all I've said. After all she's said!' His tone was dry, his flourish of hand and eyebrows faintly humorous. Marjorie nodded. A hatred of children had been recently cited as one of the main things they held in common.

'I do want a baby,' Helen said. 'Is that so very outrageous for a . . . for a married woman of my age?'

'What would you do with it all day long? What honest use can you say it would be?'

'That's not how babies work, you idiot.'

'She hasn't thought it through.'

'I have.'

'You don't know the first thing about babies. What they eat for instance. You don't even know that, do you?'

'Yes I do. Of course I do.'

'What?'

'They eat milk, sterilised milk and those soft biscuit things. Rusks. So there.'

Mark Braintree was shaking his head.

'Anyway, you don't have to be an expert before you start. You can pick it up as you go along. Trial and error. I can read books about it. Everyone has to learn somehow. I'll ask my mother.'

'God help it then.'

'What's that supposed to mean?'

'Your mother's idea of child-rearing began and ended with the nanny bureau. You've said so yourself.'

'Thanks for pointing that out.'

'I don't think you even know what a baby is.'

'What?'

'You heard.'

'You just don't like people. That's your problem.'

'What do you think a baby is, Mark?' Marjorie asked. 'It's an extremely good question.'

'It's trouble, that's what it is.'

'Only sometimes,' Helen countered. 'Babies can be difficult but a lot of the time it's the best thing in the world.'

'What do you think?' Mark asked Marjorie. 'Do you think we should have a baby? D'you think we're up to the job?'

'Would you give us a reference?' Helen giggled.

Marjorie gave a graceless jolt in her seat, which left her
skirt half-way up her thighs. She smoothed it down quickly
and tugged at her blue-and-white striped sleeves. Her eyes
fixed fully on Mark Braintree in his perfectly ironed shirt, then
moved gradually on to his wife, who was still giggling anxiously.
'I'm quite startled by this new development, I must say. We
seem to have raced from whether you two genuinely want to
have a future together to the idea of starting a family. Mark,
you began the session in a manner that was very dismissive of
Helen's wanting a baby, as though it was something you were
certain that you yourself did not want.'

'Well, I suppose other people manage it, don't they?' Mark
answered thoughtfully. 'Other people who are, shall we say,
ambivalent, imperfect, juvenile, prone to hysteria.'

'Thank you so much.'

'Not at all.'

'I suppose, Mark, what it would be helpful to establish is
whether you see yourself as ambivalent about the question
rather than set against it.'

'I think that's what I feel. Today.'

'And Helen?'

'I know we don't always see eye to eye, but that's no
reason for the world to say people like us could never have
a child.'

'Does it seem the world is saying it?'

'Well, you're saying it, aren't you? Looking at us as if we're
both complete loons.'

'That's not an impression I'm aware of transmitting, and
I'm sorry if that's how it came across. It just seems that only
last week you were talking about leaving Mark and now you've

been captivated by the idea of a baby. I feel we need to think about what a baby would mean for you both and also what a baby might represent. I suppose all I'm really saying is that there's a lot to talk about.'

'I agree, but sometimes, I think, in life, it pays to jump in. It might be just what we need.'

'What would be in it for the baby, though?' Marjorie did not say.

The afternoon sun was wan now, drained of all its strength. Marjorie saw a thick partition of dark light hovering in the air between her and her charges. She felt and heard a ringing in her ears and was aware of a creeping numbness travelling along her arms and legs. Her stomach was churning wildly and she did not know how to feel her proper self. A thin, prickling chill ran across her chest. She glanced at her watch. She thought of the dark, uncared-for communal stairway in May's new home, the synthetic, vomit-coloured hall carpet strewn with lint and dirt and old telephone directories and failed post. It was time for the session to end. Suddenly she knew she was going to be sick. Uncertainly she gabbled some closing words at the Braintrees.

'She's afraid we're going to go off and cook one up tonight.' Mark laughed. 'Aren't you?'

Marjorie stood up abruptly. 'Do excuse me, won't you?' With her hands covering her mouth, she bolted out of the room. Her head suspended over the toilet bowl in the cloak-room, her hand clutching her hair away from her mouth, Marjorie made a mental note: Perhaps the Braintrees just need to adopt some kind of acceptable-to-both-parties paradigm for getting on with each other. Then they'll be OK. She wiped her face and sloshed some tap-water round her mouth. 'Don't we all?' she said blackly. 'Don't we all.'

That evening at six forty-five Marjorie looked on, appalled, as Rose Dempsey prepared to make the biggest mistake of her life. Rose was wretched. It had been a horrific week. A favourite patient under her care – she had grown close to the whole family – had died suddenly and, within an hour, accusations of bad practice were flying through the ward. She had stood trembling while the senior obstetrician catalogued the errors in steely tones, his eyes brilliant with scorn, his finger wagging aggressively, although Rose knew and we knew that not one of the important decisions had been of her making.

There were other contributing factors, of course, that could be taken into account, if you wished to explain Rose's crazy new departure. The previous weekend there had been a huge row with her mother, who despaired that her daughter would ever marry and accused her of holding herself – mistakenly, it was implied – in too high esteem. Also, there was the small matter of her promotion. Having been clearly given the impression by her immediate superior that the position of senior staff nurse was hers, the appointment had been made and Jenny had proved the successful candidate. The upshot of all these events was that on Friday night she had been bought one too many gin-and-grapefruits by Dr Hardy in the Feathers and had hastily agreed to become his wife.

It was clearly madness. Everyone warned her against it. One by one they traipsed up to the little glass nurses' station or to the pantry where the tea urns and stacks of grey-green saucers were kept, or to the locker area or to the dimly lit car park and tried to talk her out of it.

Some were coy: 'He's too different from you.'

'Oh, I wouldn't mind that,' she said.

Others were more forthright: 'He's never been faithful to a woman in his life. What makes you think you'll be different?'

'Why, because he's never been married before. He's never had me to come home to,' came her smart retort.

Marjorie was incensed. It was so out of character. 'No! No! No!' she shouted at the television. Rose was a cautious person. Three weeks earlier she had admitted to Nurse Angela that she couldn't ignore all the rumours about Dr Hardy. That she believed him to be, in some fundamental way, unreliable. She wouldn't be so stupid, would she? To Angela's kindly warnings Rose pleaded loneliness. To wake up with someone every day, she said. Imagine the joy. Angela would not allow it. She shook her head. Nothing lonelier than being with someone who doesn't understand you.

'But I'm not so very hard to understand,' Rose said. 'I'm an open book! And if we're blessed and children come along . . .'

But the audience knew, and Marjorie in particular because she had once or twice thought it over – in fact, she had assumed that Rose knew too – that Bob Hardy did not want a family. One of three brothers who had fought like dogs, he had taken a vow never to have children. He had even gone to the trouble, as a young man, of having a vasectomy. 'I can't believe you haven't discussed it,' Marjorie shouted at the screen, incredulous, exhilarated. 'He should have told you.'

She was shaking her head from side to side. 'He should have let you know. Talk about bad omens.'

The wedding was going to be a grand affair. Hardy's parents had a country mansion. There was to be a ceremony in the village church and then a reception, with dinner and dancing in a striped marquee.

'What's your hurry?' Marjorie murmured sadly to herself. 'Why the big rush?' Where had all the good sense gone, the wise caution, the self-sufficiency? Why had they distorted Rose's character in this way?

Marjorie reached for the phone and dialled her daughter's number. 'Maisie, she's not actually going to go through with it, is she?'

'Mum, it's only TV. You just have to remember that every year they need a wedding to boost the ratings and this year it's Rose's turn.'

'I hate it. It makes me feel so sad. Do you think genuinely sound people are capable of doing such stupid, thought-less things?'

'We-ell, I think they are, but that's a completely different thing, isn't it?'

'I suppose. But this wedding, I can't explain, it just makes me sad — not for Rose because, obviously, she doesn't exist but . . . I can't explain exactly but I can't bear people throwing themselves away on people who don't, who don't even— Oh, I don't know. It actually makes me feel betrayed. D'you think I'm mad? I feel so let down.'

May was silent. There was a lengthy pause and then a voice came, still and hard: 'OK. What is this really about, Mum?'

'What?'

'If you've got something to say just—'

Marjorie stumbled for an answer. 'I don't know what you mean. I know it's stupid but it's like I'm losing a friend somehow. I just can't believe anyone could be so— I really didn't mean anything more—'

'Because if you're saying what I—'

'It's nothing like that, I swear.'

'Well, you know because—'

'You don't need to police me like this. Surely I'm allowed my foolish opinions about the television?' she did not say.

'Look, I'll see you on Tuesday. I've got to go, OK?'

What was wrong with everybody? Experience had taught her that during unexpected warm spells people were always more exaggerated in their behaviour, more confused, angrier, more amorous, even, but this was ridiculous. At work she'd seen men with eyes like volcanic rock, and women who confessed that the minute their husbands' backs were turned their hands formed claws, all poised for attack.

One patient, happy in a fish restaurant on a Saturday night, in drink, announced to his girlfriend (his wife was away on a conference), 'But of course you must keep the baby. Just think. A little baby!' but on Monday morning, in the grimy office coffee shop, his fingers grinding dry toast into crumbs as he spoke, he just said, 'Sorry. No. It's just not something we can do right now. Maybe in a year or two.' Could he bring his girlfriend to a session while his wife was away? He wouldn't mind a second opinion. Should he, after all, jump ship? Was there a standard way of not hurting anyone? Procedures? Damage limitation? 'I can't sleep,' he said. 'Should I cut down on my coffee intake?'

(Was it shameful that May's favourite food at two had been bread and butter with sugar? Ought Marjorie to apologise for this? That really was the thin end of things.)

Marjorie slumped into her favourite chair, her head heavy and clotted with a hundred separate aches. Then, from below, there came a huge crash. Frank. It was too much. She decided to go down immediately and take him to task. She banged her forearms against the locked door at the back of the passage that connected the two dwellings. 'Frank! Frank!' she cried. 'It sounds like there's a herd of elephants down there.'

Frank came thundering up the stairs – she could hear him on the other side of the party door. 'What is it? What's the matter?'

'Can you please, please, for once in your entire life—'

'Hold on. Let me just— I can't hear a word.'

She waited a few seconds until she heard Frank return, jangling a bunch of keys. Suddenly the door was open and he was facing her. He was holding a half-eaten cheese sandwich and there was green paint on his ear. 'What's the matter, Marjorie?'

Marjorie opened her mouth, but all that came out was a long, low groan that sounded exactly like a cow mooing.

'Marjorie? Please! Has something happened? Has there been bad news? Shall I come up?'

She shook her head and, to her dismay, it would not stop shaking, but Frank was already crashing round her sitting room. 'I'll make tea,' he said. As he busied about clumsily with cups and spouts, she imagined him making some appalling comment, such as 'We're just like an old married couple, are we not?' Instantly she felt a stab of guilt. He would not be so indelicate.

He knew the score. They sat drinking their drinks calmly, discussing such things as the portrait of a red mullet Frank had embarked on, against the clock, as it were. 'You haven't caught a whiff of anything, have you? No? Thank heavens for that. It's this blasted weather.'

Marjorie choked on her drink sending the hot liquid up the back of her throat and out through her nostrils. She mopped her lap with her sleeves. Would he never leave? Was that it now? Were they Marjorie and Frank, Frank and Marjorie for all time?

'I expect we should go to bed now,' Frank said, moments later, when both their cups were drained. He stood up, put the cups neatly on the table, saucer on saucer, cup on cup.

'*What?*' Marjorie sprang back, her cheeks blazing, her arms flapping wildly at her sides. But Frank was merely patting the back of her chair fondly and disappearing down the stairs into his flat. 'Of course, you know where I am, don't you, if you need anything ever of any sort at all at any future point?'

It was four a.m. Marjorie was wide awake. She peered at the ceiling, trying to bore and soothe herself to sleep by turn. 'Okey-dokey, okey dokey,' she crooned to herself. 'You're only human,' she said. She found it a strangely comforting thought. She leafed through a file that lay on her night table. She had a new referral the following day. A couple in their thirties, the GP's scribbled notes said. Mr and Mrs Blake. 'Wife martyr type. Obese. High blood pressure. Violent mood swings the norm. Hypersensitive. Repressed anger. Suggestion of paranoia. Husband seems fine.'

She cast the notes aside. If she slept now, rose at ten and

beetled into work for her eleven o'clock she would be all right. Marjorie fell asleep at five, imagining Rose Dempsey in her wedding dress, complete with nurse's hat, lace-ups and an upside-down watch pinned above the breast dart, like a little clockwork buttonhole.

The next morning on the walk to work a young girl in a brown-and-white striped school shirt stared at Marjorie as she waited at the lights to cross the road. 'Don't do it, Rose!' she yelled. 'You're worth more,' she added.

'Thanks,' Marjorie mouthed. And then, although it seemed inadequate, 'I hear what you're saying.' Later on an office window-cleaner, suspended forty feet up in a wood and rope cradle, waved at her from on high and whistled a snatch of the *Nightingale Park* theme tune in her direction. Under her breath Marjorie murmured the words to his wobbly accompaniment:

> *All the world has troubles,*
> *All the world's been hurt,*
> *I can heal your worries,*
> *Let you know what you are worth.*
> *Together we'll find happiness,*
> *Together we'll be saved,*
> *And till that time you know I'll never*
> *Let you hurt again.*

Two black nuns walked briskly past her, then turned to examine her face from the street corner while they waited for the lights to change. They nudged each other and giggled, clasping their black leather bags to their chests. But the laughter was without mirth. There was horror in it. But, then, perhaps all marriage seemed to them a vastly dangerous adventure, alien, and as painful and risky as heart surgery.

That morning Richard had called a branch meeting. The five most senior counsellors who worked at the Wellbeck were seated in a semi-circle with their boss at the crown of the arc. Audrey, the secretary, was taking the minutes. Richard handed out a roughly typed agenda. By way of introduction he sighed and said, 'It's funding problems again. It may no longer be possible for us not to charge clients. There's been a suggestion that we introduce a sliding scale of fees and I need to know your thoughts.'

There were nods of agreement round the circle. Marjorie peered at the faces: the eyes, the mouths, the noses.

'If we have to charge we have to charge.'

'And it's not necessarily a tragedy either. I personally have two sets of clients who often don't turn up. There's no way that would happen if they were paying for the counselling.'

'I sometimes feel I would be appreciated more if my clients paid me. They would take me more seriously.'

'This will sound pathetic but I think it would be good for my self-esteem!' There was general merriment at this.

'I think they'd make more effort in the sessions. Put more in. Match the cash investment with extra commitment. It's basic market forces.'

'What do you think, Marjorie?'

'It's bad enough that people have to come here, without having to pay for the privilege. I'd rather — I don't know — I'd rather make a contribution myself than have my clients pay to see me. It would alter everything. I think it's obscene! We're not doing them a favour. The whole thing's a collaboration, surely. They do just as much work as we. More, usually. We can't ask them to pay,' she did not say.

'I imagine you feel very strongly.' Richard turned to face her.

She nodded. 'I wouldn't want to work under those conditions.'

'Well, thank you for making that clear.'

Marjorie's face was burning. She felt six pairs of eyes glaring at her with amused alarm.

Five minutes later Mr Blake entered the room, his pink baby face giving nothing away. He was plainly dressed, apart from scuffed black cowboy boots and a heavily studded belt. A smell came from him that was slightly faecal. His wife followed behind him, trailing long black skirts. She stopped in front of her allocated chair, her head drooped, shuffling her feet in their puffy white running shoes, making silent calculations. For an awful moment Marjorie thought that Mrs Blake might not fit her seat. But presently she turned her back to the room, grabbed both arms of the chair, peered up at Marjorie, turned away her gaze again and then, very, very slowly, she lowered herself down and positioned her large form, with its accompanying swathes of black jersey material, as gracefully as possible inside the chair. Although there was not much space to spare, and there was a slick of sweat on her forehead, and the breaths she took were short and close, she did not seem uncomfortable. She let out a sigh of achievement, then smiled up appreciatively at Marjorie, mouthing, 'Thank you.'

Marjorie returned the smile instantly.

'There's no nice way of saying it,' Mr Blake began.

'Are you quite, quite sure?' Marjorie did not say.

'Our marriage is being threatened by my wife's size.' He gave an amused little snort. 'She's crushing me. Literally. It's not pleasant. I mean, you should see what she eats. You would not believe . . .' He moved his hands far apart to indicate volume.

Mrs Blake's head was nodding up and down. 'It's true,' she said simply. 'After the twins were born everything went pear-shaped. I know there's no excuse.'

'I mean, I love her to bits, do anything for her, but would you want to wake up next to . . . ?'

Mrs Blake's nodding grew swifter. 'I really am a liability, aren't I?'

'A figure of fun, you see, is what I'm becoming. You'd never guess but she wasn't bad-looking when we got together. No oil painting, but you knew you could walk down the street with her without having to, you know, without people calling us names, without the shame of it all. What I'm trying to say is, we weren't always looked on as freaks.'

'It's true.' Mrs Blake gave a small, reminiscing sigh. 'People used to leave us alone.'

'We've tried every diet under the sun, haven't we, pet? She just can't stick to them, can you? Never had any sort of self-control.'

'I do find it hard, I have to say. I've always been weak-willed.'

'I've done my bit. "I'll swear off chocolate if you do," I say. We have baked potatoes and salad for dinner and fresh fruit cocktail, then what do I find stuffed inside an old Tampax box in the back of the bathroom cabinet? A king-size Mars and a steak and kidney pie. It's disgusting, really.'

'I do admit I have a problem.' Mrs Blake looked up helpfully.

'Yeah, you're a flaming greedy pig – sorry, love. But we've got to face facts. It's the only way.'

'It's true. I wake up in the morning and think, I'll be really good today, and I have a grapefruit for breakfast and some wholewheat toast with just a scrape of marge and then I'll have carrot sticks for my mid-morning with a glass of hot lemon water, and at lunchtime I'll have a bowl of soup and a turkey sandwich and a low-fat yoghurt, and then for dinner I'll have, I don't know, maybe some cod in parsley sauce with boiled potatoes and unlimited greens and a diet cola, and I'll do five minutes on the abdominiser we've got in the garage, and then I think I'll just pop to the shop for the evening paper, and the next thing I know I'm in a kind of trance, and when I come out of it there's ten or twenty chocolate wrappers and an empty family-size packet of salt and vinegars on the passenger seat and I don't remember a single thing about it, and all I'm thinking is, Where was I when all that got eaten?'

'Makes me sick just thinking about it.' Mr Blake was shaking his head.

Mrs Blake bit her lip. 'I don't really know what to do,' she said. 'We're all like this in my family. Big build.'

'At school they used to call her Lardy Pants. Says it all, doesn't it? She's got to give up the pies, hasn't she? I mean, look at you.' Mrs Blake smiled and bit her lip again. 'It's not funny, love. It's nothing to smile about.'

'I'm terrible,' Mrs Blake said, trying not to giggle. 'I'm a disgrace.'

'It sounds like what you're saying is, you eat compulsively without wanting to or meaning to, or even fully knowing that you're doing it.'

'I'm not proud of myself. I just don't know what else to do.'

'I wonder if we might think a little about what it is that makes you feel compelled to eat when you don't wish to?'

'I'm just greedy, I suppose.'

'It's as simple as that.'

'But it doesn't sound as though you get much pleasure out of the food.'

'That's right. I don't even taste it half the time. It just takes me out of myself for a minute.'

'Takes your mind off the things that you find difficult?' She nodded. 'Could we try to think about what those things are?'

'Well, I get a lot of back pain, because of my size, and then I get a bit depressed sometimes because I can't keep up with the children when we're playing because I get out of breath, and then it gets Bill down, me being so large. You know,' she said brightly, 'he doesn't really deserve to—'

'She does need to shift the weight, don't you, doll?' Mr Blake gave his wife an affectionate play-kick on the shins.

'He's right,' Mrs Blake concurred. 'It's just I can't see a way out.'

'I know it's hard, but if you eat like a pig, well, it makes sense that you'll turn into a p—'

'Mr Blake, would you mind just listening for a moment or two while I ask your wife one or two things? Then

I'll ask you for your thoughts afterwards. Would that be all right?'

'Sure. Be my guest, love.'

'Thank you. Now, can you see areas of tension in the marriage that aren't related to your weight problem?'

'I don't know. I'm not sure I understand.'

'Do you feel the way you relate to each other as a family is—'

'Oh, yeah.' She shifted nervously in her seat. 'I've no complaints. I know it's my fault and that I've got a lot of changes to make but—'

'What sort of changes do you want to see?'

'Well, I suppose we don't have that much married life because of my size and—'

'Can you blame me? I mean—' he laughed '—to be honest with you – I mean apart from the physical impossibility would *you*—'

'Mr Blake! Please!' Marjorie roared suddenly, and her voice sounded so loud and emphatic that she made herself start up in her seat.

'What?'

'Stop. Just please stop talking. You did agree.'

'Steady on. No need to wet your knickers. I just thought you might like to know a couple of things. At the moment I've got the keys to the food cupboards and there's a lock on the fridge and we've drawn up a chart with her daily allocations – but she can't stop pigging out when I'm not around.'

'It seems to me that the pair of you are using the issue of weight to—'

'I don't want to be rude, Miss, but we don't really need

any of the psycho mumbo-jumbo. I just want to know how on earth I'm meant to shift the weight off her. Can't chain her up all day, can I? We could try wiring her teeth but she'd only go and hook herself up to a double-cream drip the minute our backs were turned.'

And then Mrs Blake was a ball of shame, apologising wildly, her large, trusting face convulsed with remorse. There were tears and mucus and sweat glistening on her face. She was sobbing uncontrollably. 'I just – I just – feel so terrible for putting you through all this, B-B-Bill,' she sobbed. 'I know you don't deserve it. I know I'm using up your valuable time, Miss, I'm sure there's much more deserving people out there and I'm so sorry I just – can't seem to, and I'm such a waste of space – I don't deserve to – and the worst – the worst – the worst – thing is it's so much space I'm wasting – it's so much. But I just can't and I don't know how, and I'm just so sorry about everything and—' She buried her head in her chest, collapsing into a heaving, sobbing mass of hair and bone-white neck and black fabric.

Marjorie took several breaths and quickly rehearsed one or two responses in her head. 'Mr Blake, I feel that the way you are expressing your attitude towards your wife's weight is inappropriate because it seems to me wholly lacking in sympathy.' That wasn't right. 'Mr Blake, can we look at some of the ways you have just referred to your wife within this session and try to glean from them ways in which your wife's weight problem is something to which both of you are contributing, one that serves other dynamics that exist below the surface of your marriage, matter of control, matters of mutual respect.' No, that wasn't it either. She made a few more calculations.

'Mr Blake, while you are in this room I need to point out that you must address your wife in a more respectful manner. Otherwise I am not going to be able to work with you both.' Bit prim, but it wasn't bad. She tried to improve it. She was running out of time. 'Listen, how can your wife be intimate with you, about her feelings, if there isn't going to be any sympathy?' Nearly . . . nearly . . .

Mr Blake had started up again. 'Even her own mother calls her a useless lump. I mean, what does that tell us? I can't look at her when she eats. She's a human dustbin, if you think about it, really, aren't you, pet?'

The Blakes needed her help, but the stretch she would have to make, it was just too much. Shrill little echoes from the last few weeks were playing in Marjorie's head. *The stupid thing is she wasn't even attractive, Jean wasn't. Bony old thing, really, but with loose-fleshed arms. There was no pleasure in it, not for me in any case.* But she would take the news of the wedding to heart — to her it was a terrible defection.

Eight weeks ago I was lying in the gutter outside our flats in a pool of vomit, no job . . . and the doctor gave me six months to live, two years tops.

Well, you were a lot more fun to be with then.

With intense regret she saw her daughter eking out her dinner from half a midget jar of baby food. The things people said. The things people wanted. It had been a long, lowering month. The autumn sky was pale brown, studded with ash-coloured clouds, the air clogged with a kind of unnatural heat. It was moody weather, dry and leaden. The feeling in the clinic was tense and discontented, as if everything was waiting to break. Sometimes it astonished her quite how angry the world was, its loathing and mistrust as vile and livid as vomit. Both light and dark speech had been more brutal than was usual. Was it the uncertainty of the weather? And they didn't know what they wanted, these fuming couples, on the whole, they just felt lack, like a huge and thankless hole swallowing them up. Proudly they heaped their unsayable losses at Marjorie's feet. They were furious with history for one thing. Nobody, I mean NOBODY, knows what I have to put up with.

'Well, how can they, if you won't tell?' Marjorie wanted to say.

The complacency that people brought to bear on their suffering. The commitment to it. The attention paid, daily, to the exact preserving of all its elements. The lively servicing of all the old wounds. How intensely people felt about the half-life. Of course, next week everything might change – these things went in waves. But for now why was the plain sense of things so hard to hold? It was like an allergy. The heavy industry people made of each other. Why did they feel compelled to do it? Marjorie did not know. Could they genuinely find no delight, no fellow feeling, no tolerance, even? A sensation rose in her that was like despair, but with the heart knocked out of it. It was blunter than despair, less personal. A sort of violent distaste crossed with hopelessness and insomnia.

Mr Blake was still talking. Had he not been sitting there for several hours? 'Did I tell you about the time I came back from the club and caught her picking baked beans out of the rubbish and there's tomato sauce on her chin and burned toast round her gob and scraps of potato peel up and down her arms and her hands were filthy with all kinds of revolting trash and she was in her underwear, which is never a pretty sight, and I just thought to myself—' He shook his head from side to side, but his eyes were brilliant with flashes of deranged relish. Mrs Blake's heaving, agonised sobs shook the whole room.

Just then, involuntarily, Marjorie shot out of her seat, her arms flailing about her. She turned abruptly to Mr Blake, but she could not meet his face with this degree of loathing burning in her eyes so instead she swung her gaze to his cowboy boots. They were nasty in the extreme, with their crass little tooled flourishes, their metal suggestions of casual brutality. They disgusted her. 'GET OUT!' she screeched.

'Beg your pardon?'

'GET OUT NOW. People as vile as you don't deserve to be alive!'

Mr Blake's eyes bulged in their sockets. He snorted and a broad spray of his saliva flew across the room and settled on the carpet next to Marjorie's shoes. *'What?'* he boomed. 'I'm not standing for this!' He sprang to his feet.

'I must say, I don't think that's very professional, Miss.' Mrs Blake frowned. Marjorie's outburst had somehow helped her regain composure. 'He's not that bad.' She looked hurt. 'Come on, Bill. Lady's obviously had a long day. We'll give her a chance to cool down, shall we? Not to worry. I'm sure she didn't mean anything. I know I'm not always the easiest person in the world to – it's probably my— We'll see you next week. You take it easy now, won't you, dear? Go and have a nice cup of tea, all right? She's probably overworked, Bill. Get yourself a treat. A nice bun or something.'

Marjorie walked briskly away from the Centre. She knew that what she had done was wrong but 'You're only human,' she said out loud, as her pace quickened, and she made certain not to catch even a glimpse of her reflection in the shop windows she passed. You are only human. Her weary feet in their thin-soled overtly feminine shoes, which lacked the support she needed, smarted against the hot pavement. For a horrible moment she felt she possessed the feet of a man in drag. She fixed her eyes on the pale, realistic noon that stretched out broadly in front of her. She saw a pre-pubescent girl with (already) a matronly figure and middle-aged attire, and near to her a frayed-looking red-haired woman, who checked herself in a silver compact, was frowning unkindly. Marjorie moistened her lips as though they were about to part and release speech but all her thoughts were violent and unspeakable.

How did you get out of your life?

Marjorie began to cry as her feet carried on walking, relentless, taking forward her shame. How did you extricate yourself from all the bad stories? Sometimes people felt like colossal failures just because it was the first time their spouse had left the haemorrhoid cream on the night table or the preparation for athlete's foot. And failure made them murderous, swinging viciously from their hinges All the people around her seemed so intent on looking after their own history. But how did they know if their pleasure was real or their pain?

She paused at the baker's and read the postcards in the window. Among the three-piece suites for sale and the toaster (boxed, unused, buyer collects), she read, 'TEMPORARY HOUSE-KEEPER WANTED FOR 2 WEEKS FROM 2–16 OCTOBER (WIFE GOING AWAY) LUXURY APARTMENT – LIVE IN.' Marjorie scribbled down the number and scuttled off home.

Seven

On the morning of Marjorie's wedding, Declan gathered up her hair in his elegant fingers and twisted it into a French pleat, shifting his weight on to his right leg and bending his neck the better to observe her in the rectangular bevelled mirror opposite. He shook his head, dropped the hair and swept it up again at a different angle so that it looked softer, less severe. He seemed remote, feminine, immersed in matters she did not fully understand. She felt their roles were reversed – was it not she who should have suggested secrets and mystery today of all days?

The salon was very carefully lit with golden low-voltage up-lights, which lent to the proceedings an air of romance. Declan was still silent. 'What are you thinking? What's wrong?' Marjorie considered asking. 'Don't you think I'll make a convincing bride?' She felt dissatisfied, physically, with herself. Her calves were troubling her. From the side, reflected in the mirror, they looked bloated and the pocket of flesh behind her right knee, where her legs had been crossed, was radish red.

Declan sucked on his bottom lip, which was thick and

low-slung. 'It all depends on how you want to be, what exactly we're going for. With the hair and makeup, you see. Do you want to look powerful, sexy, sweet, vulnerable . . . ?'

Definitely not vulnerable. 'Is there a book I could look at?' she thought of asking, to see what the different words meant in terms of actual . . . but she kept quiet. In a tiny voice she suggested, 'Natural?'

'Oh, don't worry, I won't make you look like a Russian air hostess.'

Her sister Belinda had insisted she have professional hair and makeup for the big day. 'My treat. He's very good. Worked wonders for Caroline when she got married. A real transformation. He can do miracles. Literally.'

'Oh!'

Declan was coming at her eyelashes with a tiny sharp-spoked brush. His head loomed large, his teeth, his hands and nose, his mouth. She nearly jumped out of her skin. He looked at her curiously. 'You OK?'

'OK. Just a bit . . . you know . . .'

His manner was gentler now. He had responded kindly to something acute inside her. She saw that somehow she had become for him a real person. 'I've got it now.' He beamed. 'Oh, yes. No need to worry.' And suddenly it did not feel as though he was rubbing the character out of her and starting again from scratch to make bland, smooth, small features, exact and stupid. He was taking her face and, if anything, making it more like itself. Her mouth, for example, was quite wonky and he hadn't tried to even that out; if anything, he had emphasised it, with a very light black-cherry sheen that was almost exactly the same colour as her lips were, only more so. He arranged her hair quickly so that it looked rather casual, how she'd wear it in the bath, for instance, or if she'd doodled a French lady on a pad, a lady with a little dog, while talking on the telephone, and scribbled in a loose, messy but slightly elaborate hairdo. Declan pushed in three expert hairpins, promising it would not fall down, not even if she did.

'There,' he said. He put down his tubes and brushes and tidied them away into a black metal box. 'Radiant and trembly. What d'you think?'

'Not bad. Not bad at all.'

'Beautiful,' he said, and although it was very much understood between them that the word was being used to describe his workmanship, she could not fight her smiles.

The night before a vanload of wedding presents had been delivered and Marjorie was trying out thank-you letters in her head. She despaired of finding the right tone. She had been awake half the night agonising over each sentence.

A million thanks for what I can only describe as the Rolls-Royce of toasters. Toast has always been one of my favourite foods and now I'll be able to ensure expert quality control with every slice. I think it's the quickest toaster I have ever used. The canny thick and thin device means it's equally at home with muffins and crumpets as with ordinary bread, which means fancy breakfasts (and tea-times) with no burnt bits and no annoying grill-watching also. Thanks so much. It's lovely that it's got four slots so that we won't have to keep making extra batches. Please come round and have a few rounds with us soon.

Love, Hugh and Marjorie

PS Married life is suiting us down to the ground and now we can begin each morning by 'toasting' our happiness.

No, that wouldn't do.

Dear Granny Hemming
Thank you so much for the saucepan set. They really are the Rolls-Royces of the cooking-utensil world and it's so nice the way they fit inside each other for handy and efficient storage. [She'd got that bit off the manufacturer's label.]

As you know I cannot cook but with such top-notch equipment on hand I now have a reason to learn and am thinking of embarking on a course. Hugh, who knows about such things, says they really are the best you can buy and will last for a minimum of thirty years, and that's with daily use.

Next time you're in town perhaps you'll pop round and sample one of my latest 'creations'.
With love, Hugh and Marjorie.

Dear X
How we admire our new kettle! Our old one is a disgrace, all furred up with limescale and crumbs and heaven knows what, and we are sometimes greeted by quite unwelcome foreign bodies in our hot beverages, I am ashamed to say. Well – no more! What a relief to show it the door.

The model you chose makes a really excellent cup of tea. The speed-boil function ensures we never have to wait more than a minute for our cuppas and I really can't thank you enough. Without doubt it really is the Rolls-Royce

of kettles. Do come and enjoy a brew with us when next you're thirsty.
All love, Hugh and Marjorie X

Now Declan was attaching her veil. The salon became silent: chatting ceased and hair-dryers were switched on to their lowest settings as a mark of respect. This is a highly regarded ritual that does not happen every day, Marjorie thought. The veil was secured to a clear plastic comb that slotted neatly into the raised front portion of her hairdo. Declan ruffled the springy white net and arranged it in little folds down her back. He fetched her coat and carefully fed her arms through the arm-holes, smoothing down the veil and flipping it under her collar.

How could she walk down the street? How could she think of hopping onto the bus, dressed in an old navy mac and brown shoes and a great bridal headdress? But hop on the bus she did, head down thumbs rubbing against each other, for all the world like some skewed, fantasist, out-patient.

The bus conductor would not allow her any kind of low profile. 'Fancy dress party, is it, Miss?'

'No, it's, um, I'm getting married, but I had to get my hair done earlier because I didn't know how to put the veil in myself. I'm going to get changed into my dress now at the hotel and—'

'What time's kick-off?'

'Twelve o'clock.'

'D'you hear that, everyone?' the conductor boomed 'Let's hear it for this young lady who's getting married today!'

There was a generous outpouring of cheers and applause

from the lower deck. Some elderly ladies on nearby seats wished her luck, and one fished a sprig of heather in a twist of silver foil from her handbag and laid it on Marjorie's lap. Then the bus came to an abrupt halt and the driver swung out of his seat and climbed on board to see what was occurring and when he had been informed of the proceedings he planted a wet kiss on Marjorie's mouth, and on the bristly tip of his moustache she detected the unmistakable aroma of wine gums.

'Oh!' she cried.

'Traditional, isn't it?'

'I s'pose,' she mumbled, she who had only ever been kissed by one man.

On an adjacent seat a young mother undressed her baby and began changing his nappy right there on the claret-plaid plush, and a terrible smell rose up and filled the lower deck, and everyone went, 'Euuugh!' and the woman apologised moodily, repeating, 'What do you expect me to do?' and the driver took this as his cue to get back into his cab, whereupon he revved up with so much noise and smoke that, for an awful moment, Marjorie thought he was going to attempt a wheelie.

Inside the bus the festive air prevailed for a short while, with delicate and then less than delicate inquiries being addressed to the bride, but gradually the atmosphere cooled and settled, and moments later the heather lady was whispering about her youngest son's divorce. Finally Marjorie reached her stop and stepped on to the cool pavement, murmuring softly, 'Well, this is me.' The conductor gave her a highly saucy wink as she caught his eye, and for a split second she felt off-balance and forgot whether she was married yet, and why she was taking this huge leap. She peered longingly at the bus as it crawled down the high street, steely and dignified, the driver caressing the steering-wheel, Marjorie noted, through the window into his compartment, with a somewhat sensuous hand.

When Marjorie walked into work on Friday morning she came straight away face to face with Richard Adler, the director of the Centre, who looked anxious and harassed. 'Marjorie, I need to talk to you. You wouldn't have half an hour now, would you?'

Evidently it was something serious. Mr Blake must have complained, she thought. She had thrown him out of her consulting room, but it had been for his own good. She might have killed him! She had been hoping to get in her version of events first but something had held her back: a mixture of, what was it? Shame? Disbelief? She started rehearsing her lines rapidly. 'You see, almost immediately I knew I couldn't work with them. It was an overwhelming feeling I had, like a chemical reaction. It's something I regret hugely because, with the right person, they might be able to do some good work, but it was impossible for me. I couldn't remain detached. I will apologise to them formally because, as you know, it's so unlike me. I've done the draft of a letter already – perhaps I can show it to you. I should have been more careful. It wasn't that I didn't know how – it was more I just could not bear even to sit there with – I suppose I just developed some sort of instant allergy.' She would describe his vile tone, his supercilious cruelty, his violence. Those tooled boots. Surely Richard would understand. A sort of living saint himself, he would not approve but he would understand.

Richard scratched his head. 'I don't know how to tell you this, Marjorie,' he began, 'but I'm afraid this week I have received a serious complaint about your work.'

Marjorie tried to compose herself: she did not wish to rant. 'I was just coming to see you about it. I am so sorry. There really was nothing I could do. You'd have done the same. I never dislike people, not really. It's not my nature. I can get on with anyone. Like them, even. But the things he said were absolutely intolerable. The cruelty was so physical. I just felt that letting it continue in my presence was a way of colluding with it, condoning it. I just couldn't. The verbal assaults were just so – and the wife, cowering in the corner, just a ball of shame, pretty much unaware of what he was doing and apologising for existing. And if you'd seen the disgusting boots. They were the last straw. I'm so sorry, Richard. It will never happen again.'

'Marjorie, wait a moment,' Richard said. 'I don't think you're listening properly.' Her voice dwindled into a few unintelligible pleas, her arms made the open-handed gestures of a reasonable person. 'Please, Marjorie.' Richard was always courteous, honest and fair. She need not fear.

'Now,' he said, 'I've no idea what you're talking about.' He was still speaking and, in his pinkish hands, there was a pile of letters, and he was shuffling them loosely. The assorted greys and blues and whites of the leaves, with the scratchy writing or neat type or black lines, looked to Marjorie like some kind of – What was happening? She felt herself shake, her hands, her knees. In the last week she had had nineteen hours' sleep in total. Richard made a few apologetic sounds by way of an introduction, then began to read: '*To the Director of the blah blah blah, Really felt we needed to write a letter of complaint about your counsellor Mrs Hemming. While obviously an intelligent and kind woman, whom my ex-husband and I both liked very much, with hindsight I feel she had such a high investment in keeping us together, no matter what, that it skewed her professional judgement. Her priority, above all, was to save the marriage, and because of this we feel she overlooked the fact that there were vast problems in our relationship from the very beginning, even before the wedding. These huge obstacles seemed to her molehills, and while this at first was an attractive notion, it soon became distorting and distressing. When we decided to divorce and conveyed this to Mrs Hemming, we were made to feel that we had committed an act of betrayal. It was actually easier telling our eleven-year-old son that we were separating than it was telling Mrs Hemming.*'

Richard put the letter down. Then he took up another. Another! '*Mrs Hemming seems so set on keeping my husband and me married that a little problem like his constant threatening verbal abuse seems to count for nothing. What planet is she living on?*'

Richard drew a pale blue sheet of paper from his desk. '*My wife and I won't be coming for any further counselling sessions with Mrs Hemming. We both agree that our differences with her are absolutely irreconcilable – as a matter of fact it's the one thing we do agree about. We wish to separate and Mrs Hemming wishes us to stay together. Arrogant as it may seem, we feel we know what's best for us. There's really nothing more to say.*'

'People come and ask us to save their marriages, then

complain because we try. It's so unfair. You know my success rate.'

'I'm afraid that may be part of the problem. It's not a failure of yours if people wish to separate. We're not on a rescue mission. We have talked along these lines before.'

'I know.'

'You know, Marjorie, even the Samaritans aren't allowed to try to prevent someone committing suicide if they want to. They're just there to provide a lifeline to those who seek it.'

'Isn't it the same thing?'

'Well, no, they don't want to go against the will of the individual. They don't have their own personal agenda. Another letter mentions emotional blackmail.'

'How ridiculous. You know how much people project on to us.'

'I know, but even so—'

'These things are complicated. People have mixed feelings. They want to split and they want to stay together. They come to me because they want me to help them make a go of it. They say that. It says so in my notes, in their referral letters, and sometimes they find the work hard and I spell it out to them that if they just keep coming back they'll turn the corner and then—' Marjorie's voice was becoming shrill. Her hands were shaking. She knew that if Richard did not make a concession to her soon she might say something wild to stun him. She felt her powerlessness, and, like that of a child, it angered and provoked her. She considered the positions available to her: ultimatums, resignations, tantrums, a dignified withdrawal, an undignified one.

Richard was calm and kind. Possibly there was a parental

note in his voice. 'Our role is to help people learn to communicate in the best possible way in order that they can find out and take steps towards achieving what they actually want.'

'Yes, a satisfying and sustaining relationship. Do you think I don't know that?'

'Or an effective and manageable separation.'

'Only as a last resort, though! If all else fails.'

Richard smiled kindly. 'You think I'm against you, but our positions are closer than you realise. I value your work here and consider you one of our most experienced and capable counsellors.'

'Well, then!'

'I'm afraid the last letter goes on to pose one or two questions about your own experience.' Was he about to bring into the arena the subject of her own failed marriage? She had confided to him, during the training, extremely private information about her husband's death. For example—

He handed the closely typed page to her but she couldn't read what it said, the coy insinuations about her own private life, the intrusive assumptions about the ring on her wedding finger, about her religious leanings, her family life, her dress sense – the nasty little conclusions that had been drawn by people she had almost regarded, had treated, as her own relations!

She bit her lip and tried to gather herself in, largely for Richard's sake.

'The thing is, I'm afraid people like you and me, we're out of fashion. Now that the governing bodies place the emphasis on communication above everything, you see, things have changed.

In the annual notes, from last year I think it is . . .' he reached inside his desk '. . . it says, "How a couple communicates is more important than what is said—"'

'Yes, but I agree with that.'

'You do and you don't. You do view a couple who decide to separate as a personal failure, almost as a tragedy. You've told me so on more than one occasion.' Marjorie said nothing. 'You see, if you tell that to the Hearing—'

'There's going to be an inquiry? My God! When? What for? I mean—'

'It's only internal. It's just that one of these letters was copied to the board of directors and it's duty-bound to investigate every complaint because—'

'Because what?'

'Well, I was going to say, because we get them so rarely. I'm very sorry. I'm going to write them a letter supporting the work you do for us. I'm a hundred per cent behind you. If you can just think of this as a rather unpleasant thing that in two or three weeks will have probably fallen away . . .' Richard looked awkward. 'There's another thing I wanted to ask. As a friend.'

Marjorie raised her weary eyes to meet his glance.

'I do hope you don't object to my saying it, but is anything troubling you? Anything that you think I ought to know about? Anything that could, in any way, be considered by you – or by me – to be any of my business, as it were? The last thing I want to do is interfere. But these past few months you just haven't seemed yourself. I hope I'm not speaking out of turn. Do you mind my asking, just as a friend?'

'My daughter left,' Marjorie did not say. How could she name the enormous rush of love and pity, the shame-faced clawing for affection and approval and forgiveness and loyalty that you felt when you met your daughter's reasonable green eyes or when you dodged them, whenever you even tried out her brief name under your breath? The sharp vacuum left in the places where she ought to be, the places she had formerly inhabited – it was like a murder scene. The air she had dislodged with her leaving had not yet settled. It was haunted air, stale, contaminated. It was not good for a place to be characterised by what it lacked. It told on the structure of the house. Marjorie avoided the top floor, May's floor. The walls seemed wrong there, flimsy, unstable. They had too much give, and if you stared at them in the light of morning they looked loose and bulging, as though viewed through fumes. It would shock Richard – all this – he was essentially a mild person. It shocked Marjorie.

Her first ever meeting with Richard came back to her. It was when she had been called in to defend her thesis at the end of her first year of counselling training. On that grim late-spring day Richard, whom she knew only by name, fixed her with a quizzical stare.

'I'm unsure what to say to you. Your thesis was the best this year and also the worst. One of our examiners gave it a distinction and the other failed you outright. We sent it on to two external examiners and one thought it was ready for publication in a periodical as it stood, and would make quite an important doctorate without many alterations, and the other examiner dismissed it out of hand

and, I don't know if I should be repeating this, called into question—'

'Called into question?'

'The state of mind of the writer.'

'What?'

Richard hurried on: 'What troubled the examiners who took the more negative views was the fact that all the research you carried out was based on the relationships of couples in . . . well, in fiction.'

'And they had problems with that, did they?'

'Well, yes, some of them did. They felt uncomfortable that instead of drawing on clinical practice and academic findings you looked for your insights into human nature in poetry and novels. They were uneasy with the fact that you regarded the behaviour of people in books with the same degree of seriousness and importance as people in real life. That you didn't make a distinction. That, possibly, you couldn't see there was a distinction to be drawn.'

'They thought I thought the books were real?'

'That you thought they were about real people, yes.'

'You mean they thought I thought Jane Austen and Hardy were writing clinical research material for some unnamed institute for marital studies?'

'Well, I don't suppose they exactly – mean . . .'

'Did they think that Freud was confused about reality when he drew on the Greek myths?'

'Well, I'm afraid some of them probably would have done. What's important here is that we have two choices. You can defend your thesis before a small examining board, fifty per cent of which we already know to be entirely hostile to your approach, or you can resubmit it using a small amount of more conventional research material to balance the points you draw from literature.'

'What did you think of my thesis?'

'I thought it was a smashing piece of work, first class, original, full of understanding and intelligence, but I'm afraid I can't pass it as it stands.'

But that time it had been easy. She had followed Richard's suggestions and all objections had fallen away. In fact, she had been named a star. She smiled and looked up.

'Marjorie? Marjorie?' Richard was calling to her. She had forgotten she was still in his room, in his chair, on his hands. 'Are you all right? Are you feeling unwell?' he asked.

She considered the matter closely. 'Not unwell, exactly, more . . .'

Richard looked up, but to Marjorie's astonishment, she was on her feet already, looping her outdoor clothes round her roughly, pushing swathes of material against her person in the hope that they might fasten or at least lie flat or be controlled.

She was at the door now reaching for the handle. 'Can I let you know?' she said. 'Would that be all right?'

Eight

Marjorie lingered outside the entrance to the Maresfield
College and Clinic where she had been invited to explain
herself before the board of counsellors. Next to the little
grey-paved forecourt with parking beyond was a small flower-
bed municipally planted with strict rows of marigolds and
irises. It was a hideous modern building, brown brick and
angular, which made much use of tinted glass. Through
the glass doors she read the orange signs by the reception
desk where a telephonist sat gazing into space. There were
arrows pointing to the training section of the operation, the
administration department, the reference library, the lecture
hall and the clinic. A lone sentence from the Counsellors'
Ethics Handbook was playing distractedly on Marjorie's lips.
'Conduct that is regarded as "disgraceful" need not amount to
moral turpitude or be restricted to acts of serious immorality.'
Marjorie breathed out and closed her eyes. She shook her head,
painfully. Presently a couple emerged through the automatic
doors. 'Don't ever speak to me again,' the woman hissed.

'Fucking bitch,' the man retorted.

'OK,' Marjorie said to herself.

She made her way into the building and gave her name to the receptionist, spelling it out slowly. She took a seat in the waiting room, which was at the other end of a long, brilliantly lit, milk-coloured corridor where another receptionist took her name. There was no record of her appointment. Which counsellor did she usually see? Marjorie explained the situation and the woman gave her a stare, then told her to kindly wait until she was called.

In the waiting room, which was devoid of cheer, sat three couples and a single woman, who was glancing at her watch. There was an air of gross unease. No one spoke or moved or blinked, or so it seemed. After a few minutes a man sauntered into the room and greeted the lone woman coolly. Marjorie peered at him. He was wearing a striped scarf the same as one May had. There were a lot of them about, but he was dimly familiar also. An old patient, was it? How embarrassing! She hid her face in a magazine's black-and-white wordsearch puzzle. Over the tips of the pages she stole another glance. Wasn't he the man who had once sat calmly in Marjorie's chair as his wife told of her long-time infatuation with his brother? And yet the woman did not look familiar. Was he on another wife already? She should parade him in front of the disciplinary committee, as proof that she did not force everyone to paper over the cracks. Just then the man turned round to avoid a questioning stare from his partner, who seemed disappointed with him in the extreme. When he caught sight of Marjorie his face bulged with alarm and he coloured deeply and swung round from her so that his head was only two or three inches from the wall. Presently each of the couples was collected by a therapist, leaving Marjorie sitting alone. That was when she recognised him, from the back being led away, his leaden bearing, his hands stuffed defensively into the pockets of his not-quite-navy-blue suit. Marjorie took deep breaths. She couldn't take it on board just now. She thought of lying on the floor the better to recover for her imminent ordeal, but just then her name was called and she made her way down the glaring corridor that was so well lit and highly disinfected that you could have performed keyhole surgery in it, and she took her seat in the appointed consulting room and smiled calmly at the panel of four – two men and two women – who faced her gravely from behind a large desk in their stiff, unlovely clothes.

On the bus home Marjorie squinted at the headlines in her neighbour's newspaper, unwrapping a peppermint noisily as a decoy. On page three, above a picture of an elderly man in waterproofs and waders, she read, 'Married life threatened by Arctic fishermen.' Is it some kind of hormones they're giving the fish now? she wondered. Was it something wistful about the number of creatures left in the sea?

As the bus turned into the main road, she saw Frank, her lodger, traipsing back towards their street. Today there was something about him that was faintly heroic seeming, a luxuriance to his hair, a thick, generous gait, an air of agitation or impatience that vaguely suggested a passionate personality, but this was countered sharply by the fact of his skin, which was an odd sort of pale mauve hue, and thin-looking and tragic. Suddenly Marjorie had an idea that, close-up, he might be as touchy as an adolescent girl. Physically awkward, she somehow felt, and the most tentative steps towards him might mean continually treading on his toes. Occasionally when Marjorie watched him returning from work, she glimpsed his large brown eyes, smarting from some fresh schoolboy insensitivity. When they'd had their little run-in four years earlier he had once invited her into his sitting room and asked, with grinning lips, whether she'd mind if he took off his socks and shoes. Well, she did mind. It was eleven o' clock in the morning. She said so. That was quite enough of that. Still, she was not wholly unsympathetic. He was a good man.

'Guess what, Frank?' she tried out, under her breath, lively, matter-of-fact. 'I've been given a dressing-down. They've put me on probation. Going to keep a close eye on me. It seems I'm too good at my job. My success rate's too high. Apparently I've been forcing people to stay together against their will. You see, I'm a bit of a dinosaur. They don't need me any more,' she'd say, chirping it out. 'A relic. A throwback. A fly in the ointment.'

It was her stop and she mouthed goodbye to her seat-mate, taking a final glance at the newspaper. A New York politician was calling for the United States government to pay a thousand dollars to every black person in America to say sorry for the fact of slavery. It was an interesting idea. But would the payment constitute some sort of contract? And, if so, would it mean the survivors, the descendants, weren't allowed to mind any more? Was it a sanitising of history, plain old shut-up money? Marjorie did not know. And then she saw her mistake. It did not say that Arctic fishermen were threatening married life, it was *marine* life they were endangering. Well, she supposed, equably, it did make more sense. With that kind of accuracy, was it any wonder she had been shown the door?

Frank was approaching the bus stop as she climbed off, smoothing her hair and, with sleight-of-hand, disposing of her peppermint, which had grown too strong. He nodded. 'What kind of day have you had?' she asked evenly.

'We-ell,' he said. 'I can't really . . . You see . . .' He wiped his eyes on his sleeve.

'Has there been some kind of . . . disappointment?'

'Only of the most infinitesimal kind. One of the boys, one I liked, I found him being vile to another boy, a smaller boy who has a slight speech impediment — I know it's the kind of thing that happens all the time in other schools but . . .'

'But still,' Marjorie said, 'you must feel—' She stopped.

'It feels like a betrayal.'

She could not think what to say. 'And it was completely unexpected?'

'Yes. From the last person in the world you would imagine capable of such—'

'And he was saying nasty things and so on—'

'Yes, and I'm afraid there was a — a sexual element as well.' Marjorie took a sideways step, which meant she almost fell into the gutter. 'Well, possibly there was that motive. I don't know exactly how you define these things. And I think the police may have to be involved. I'm meeting with the head tomorrow, but I feel confused about everything, not just my loyalties but . . . I don't know. It's not my decision. It's out of my hands now.' Frank was trembling as he spoke and his face had turned a dry sort of stone colour.

'How completely . . . shocking.'

'Yes. Shocking's right. I think I'm in shock, as they say. You know, you're so good.' He looked up smilingly.

'Good?'

'At this sort of thing, I mean. Obviously.'

'Well, not really.' She smiled faintly. She might just drop it in now. 'Been given an official warning today. They're going to watch me closely. Monitor my work.'

'What?'

'I've been put on probation.' Marjorie sucked at her lower lip with her teeth. 'Well, as good as.' There, she had said it.

'No!' Frank was incredulous. 'But you're so – so . . . good.'

'Well, thanks very much, but I'm afraid—'

They were passing the pub on the corner, which was called The Oaks. 'You must need a drink. Please. I know I do.'

'Well . . . I'm not sure.'

But already she was inside, sitting in a booth of plum-coloured buttoned velour, which was streaked with white ash, while Frank went off to fetch drinks. The air was heavy with stale smoke and old spilt beer, and now and then there rose up the scent of a vicious lime-flavoured toilet cleaner, which made Marjorie's sinuses throb. Twin orange-glass carriage-lights cast dim little discs of light on either side of her head. Presently Frank returned with two large whiskies and a small jug of water. He placed a packet of crisps on the table, running his thumbnail down the join and teasing open the seams.

Frank drained his drink and turned to her banging his hand on the sticky table-top. It was four o'clock. 'Let me get this right.' He leaned in towards her the clearer to make his point. At once Marjorie knew it was not his first drink of the day. 'You've been disciplined for discouraging people from separating?'

'Well, I've been—'

'For trying to find ways to help people – how do you say? – to all intents and purposes rub along together.'

She nodded. 'To all intents and purposes – yes.'

'How can it be your fault if people decide to like each other more than they intended? It happens every day.'

'It's not that so much. It's more that it was felt I put pressure on people to stay together when it was not their best option. That I made them do it.'

'Really, you were able to do that?'

'It's ridiculous, the whole thing.'

'Ludicrous. It absolutely beggars belief! Do they think you are a magician of some sort?'

'Of course, to be fair, they said I did it unconsciously.'

'That's good of them.'

'My world-view, they said, was rosier than the actual world is, and because of that I'm always trying to change the world to meet my expectations of it. Apparently. I mean, how can they know a thing like that? Surely?'

'A personal attack, then – not that, were it the truth, one would find anything wrong in—'

She took a swig of her drink. Frank beckoned to the barman and, because it was quiet, he brought over two more whiskies. Frank gulped the first half of his and Marjorie took another swig of hers, without realising, this time, it was his drink she drank. She took a deep breath and gathered together tightly something that lay frayed in her heart. 'I'm afraid,' she began, 'you see . . . they . . . they . . . said, well, they implied, at least I think it's what they were getting at, that because I . . . I lost my marriage so soon after it began I was on some kind of blind mission to save everyone else's, and they wanted me to know that however many marriages I wrongly patched up it wouldn't ever bring Hugh back.'

'Hugh being your husband?'

'Yes.'

'They said that?'

'Well, I know it was what they were thinking. Yes.'

Frank was enraged. 'That's unforgivable.'

'They spelled it out in black and white. I might have blurred boundaries, they said. They implied that all of my motivation for trying to treat couples was . . . well . . . psychological.' She spat out the word.

'And what did you say?'

'What d'you think I said? I told them,' she lowered her voice, which was throaty now, theatrical, whisky-hoarse, 'to fuck off.' She made to drain her glass but it was already empty, as was his, because she had polished that off too. Frank took the hint. He came back from the bar with a bottle of Scotch, which he placed purposefully between them.

'Oh, Frank,' she said, overwhelmed by his generosity.

'This is terrible,' he murmured. 'Blow the expense.'

The pub was a little busier now. A slight woman approached Marjorie, holding out an autograph book in the dim orange light. 'It is you, isn't it?' she mouthed.

Marjorie nodded and slipped on her dark glasses and signed Rose Dempsey's name. 'We're worried about Rose,' the woman said, 'me and my sister.'

'Why's that, now?'

'She's so trusting. You can't always think the best of everyone all the time. It's not sensible. You've got to protect yourself more. Toughen up.'

'I'm stronger than I look, you know,' Marjorie countered, with a hint of flirtation.

'Are you, dear? Well, perhaps we won't worry so much, then.'

'I'm sure there's no need.'

'You mean it? Obviously you've seen the new scripts and everything. You couldn't just tell me if you actually make it down the aisle?'

Marjorie gave the woman a heartfelt look. 'I wish I knew, but we only get the scripts two days before filming and when it's a big storyline we have to sign confidentiality agreements and so on. I am sorry.' She lowered her voice, glancing round for eavesdroppers: 'I can tell you this, though,' the woman drew closer to her, 'thing is, let's just say, you and your sister have got nothing to worry about. Not long term. OK? I can't say any more, but d'you under-stand?'

'Oh, that's wonderful news. And I won't tell a soul. Take care now. God bless.'

'And you. 'Bye now.'

Frank looked on, bemused. 'What on earth—'

'It's just a little game people like to have with me. Appar-ently I'm the spitting image of someone who appears regularly on the television. I've tried to get out of it but it's simpler this way, believe me. And there's no harm,' she added, but suddenly she felt foolish and ashamed.

'I understand,' he said uncertainly.

The woman was chatting nearby to another woman who resembled her physically. 'I've always believed that what you put out in life, you get back,' she said coolly.

'Lucky you're not working on the bins, then, eh?' her companion replied, giggly, good-humoured, mildly hysterical.

'It is, of course, an absolute outrage,' Frank kept repeating, loyal to the end.

'They've also Strongly Recommended I do a refresher course and submit a written piece of work justifying my practice methods, go into personal therapy again myself with a practitioner of their choosing, and have a weekly rather than a monthly supervision with Richard, my boss.'

'And will you do all that?'

'I'm deciding.'

'Why not set up shop yourself?'

'Private practice, you mean?'

He nodded. 'Take your best people with you. I bet they'd come like a shot.'

'One or two might, but I'm not sure it would be right.'

'And you could get new people, couldn't you?'

'I suppose.'

'You could specialise in a certain field, perhaps. What do you think your strengths are, professionally?'

'Well, I don't know. I think I'm quite good at getting people to reconcile things. Not forcing them but, you know, giving them a leg up.'

'Helping people to apologise to each other, you mean.'

'Well, that's certainly part of it. And it doesn't come easily, not to most people.'

Frank was regarding the whisky bottle as something of a challenge, each drink larger and faster than the last. 'I've been thinking a lot about my father. How I wanted him to apologise for things before he died, but he never did. The strange thing was that after he died I didn't feel badly towards him any more. The bad feelings simply went away, as though his death healed something. And afterwards I had these huge feelings of . . . well, health, I suppose. But why did it take something as big as that?'

'Apologise for things that happened when you were a child, do you mean?' But Frank did not hear or was not listening. Suddenly the beginnings of the evening trade were evident all around. Two slender girls clutching pale leather bags anticipated the arrival of a third about whom they had their reservations. 'I wouldn't mind, but she didn't even fancy him, she told me. Said he reminded her of an undertaker.'

Just then a man with a beard accosted an elderly woman with a hard pat on the back, the foam on the top of his drink slapping against the rim of his glass and leaping on to her blouse. 'Sorry, Mum,' he mouthed, grinning and dabbing at her front with his cuff. 'Get off!' she shrieked. In the corner of the room a fruit machine flashed seductively, a strip of little illuminated cherries danced against a frenzied piped soundtrack. A curl of cigarette smoke drifted in front of Marjorie's eyes and she batted it away, thinking, thinking.

Frank was talking loudly over the noise of the juke-box. The bottle in front of him was more than half empty. 'Well, I don't know what I'm talking about here, absolutely no idea, but what if you set up a kind of service for people who want apologies? Want to give them or want to get them. Who don't know how. You could tell them how to go about it. Or how not to. For people who can't live their lives happily because they feel owed or owing. There's so much sorrow in the world. And shame and oppression, and someone like you could be just the person to— You could call it the . . . the Sorry Bureau – or, no, the Sorry Business. You could advertise in the local paper.'

'Well, it's a nice idea.'

'You could start small and go global. Why stop at domestic disputes? Think big! You could get the Catholic Church to apologise for not doing more to assist the Jews in the war. You could get the British establishment to apologise for crimes committed against Ireland. You could . . . you could . . . There's a lot of guilty people out there who want to make amends but don't know how, and a lot of people who aren't guilty enough by half who owe apologies and need your help to realise it.'

Marjorie took a sip from her glass. Her head was spinning gently and if she looked at things for long they danced round the room. She couldn't believe her daring. She had never drunk this much in her life. 'You know what, Frank?' she slurred. 'I've done some dreadful things myself.'

'It's not possible.'

'And not a soul knows about it, but if they did . . . Things that would make anyone who knew loathe me for ever.'

'You're wrong about that. With you, Marjorie, what you forget – what I'm trying to say is, with a person like you, your so-called weaknesses are, in fact, your strengths.'

She smiled. 'That's a wonderful thing to say.'

'It's the truth.'

'You know how to make a person feel good.'

'You are good. And you mustn't forget, whatever it is, your life hasn't been an enormous bed of roses exactly, has it?'

'Well—'

'I mean, I know your daughter's brought you a great deal of comfort but—'

Something crashed behind the bar, a whole case of miniature mixer bottles, and suddenly the floor of the pub was covered with pools of sticky orange liquid and glass shards, and there was cursing and thick-bristled brooms were sweeping and hands were wrapped round dustpans, and there were clumps of damp newspaper, and detergent and cloths and dark boots and slim ankles in high shoes, dancing to dodge the debris. Marjorie started to cry. She poured whisky into her mouth as some sort of salve but it had the reverse effect. She felt her throat on fire. She coughed and choked, and a gobbet of phlegm flew out of her mouth across the table and on to the knee of Frank's grey flannel trousers and she was so thoroughly mortified that, without stopping to think, she snatched up her bag and raced out of the pub, and ran away as fast as she could from Frank and her home and her life.

After a few minutes, drunk and out of breath and sagging, she staggered on to a passing bus, crashed her way upstairs and slumped against the back seat. She made a brief survey of her surroundings: there was a woman knitting grey wool, a man fiddling with a long-lensed camera and a schoolboy cleaning his glasses with some scraps of kitchen paper. Then everything went dead.

Three hours later Marjorie opened her eyes to utter darkness. She was alone on the top deck, shivering, bathed in sour sweat. All around was silent and deserted. The air was frozen. She clutched her ribs and shut her eyes again, but it was no good. She woke gradually, stretching stiff limbs, growing alive to the disgusting smells around her, feeling her vision increasing fractionally, thanks to some distant lighting in the depot and a flickering street-lamp nearby. The claret-coloured bus seat, with the thin green and yellow columns, like some kind of accountancy stationery, reeked, and when she looked closely next to her she saw a little luminous pool of vomit. She did not even know if it was hers. The roof of her mouth was caked with something thick and dry and bitter, as if all the low-grade fat she had ever consumed had gathered there to make its home. She sniffed sadly, inhaling stale whisky on her collar and night fumes in her hair. She flexed her toes, which were sticky and damp in their stockings. Her head was stunned and muffled with a sharp core of pain, stinging with recriminations and disappointments and buried sorrows.

She saw May when she was a tiny baby, screaming in the early hours of the morning, as she did most nights, her angry red face refusing the breast, thrashing away from Marjorie's embrace, her limbs livid and despairing, her little fists beating Marjorie's throat when she crooned a lullaby or softly spoke a rhyme. When she took May into her bed, laying her on her chest to sleep, the screams grew louder than ever so she'd walk her round the house to soothe her, trying the different positions in the book, going up- and downstairs or jigging about. Failing that she would wheel her along the narrow hall in her pram to soothe her. Once May screamed solidly for seven hours. She peered through eyes slitted with loathing at Marjorie as if she were the wrongest possible person. There was only one explanation. She wanted her father.

Marjorie was so exhausted from these embattled nights that she pared herself down in order to survive. She wore the same pair of shapeless overalls for seven weeks. She ate nothing but the packets of cheese and orange juice the milkman brought. One night when May did sleep briefly Marjorie grew feverish and started seeing things. And then in the morning she fed May some puréed carrot, changed her nappy, put her to the breast, placed her in the little white cot asleep and left her, just like that. She went out walking. The whole day stretched in front of her. There were seagulls celebrating with her in the sky. She had some bacon in a café surrounded by traffic wardens. She leafed through a magazine and attempted the crossword puzzle, thinking, This is what my life would be like if— On a park bench a man asked for her phone number but she said, no, she was a Bit Involved. The day passed in a flash. She did not give her child a thought, or her dead husband. She was a single girl on a break from the waxworks. Ten hours later she turned the key in her front door thinking, vaguely, Oh. Gingerly she climbed the stairs to May's room. May lay still in her cot. No noise came from her whatsoever, but her eyes were wide open. When she saw Marjorie she blinked, but still no sounds came. Her clear, open face was without expression. Marjorie picked her up and changed her nappy, which was leaking piss and shit. She bathed her daughter and changed the bedclothes, awkwardly, with May in her arms. Still no sounds came. Marjorie fed her some more carrot and put her to the breast where she fed for three hours, her entire body trembling continuously in her mother's arms until she fell asleep. In the morning May lay silently on the carpet amid her toys, completely still, occasionally closing her eyes for a minute or two, then opening them again. It was clear that something had broken.

Marjorie winched herself out of the seat and down the little spiral steps and out into the cool night. There was no activity in the bus depot, just long phalanxes of red buses and the scent of diesel. She had no idea where she was and she threaded her way on to the main road, checked her purse for cash, and when she saw the heroic light of a taxi chugging towards her, she held out her arm and asked the driver for her street.

Much later, after a bath and toast and another bath, she sat in her dressing-gown watching a programme called *Women Scorned* on the TV. 'My husband used to drive me so crazy,' one woman announced proudly, 'that every morning before he got up I used to run his toothbrush under the rim of the toilet bowl, just to show him I wasn't his doormat.'

'I used to put bleach in a plant spray whenever I was ironing his best clothes so they used to have nasty little marks all over them when he put them on.'

'Well, I used to mix tablespoons of chilli powder in with his pickle when I did him a ploughman's for his packed lunch so he'd have the runs all day at work.'

At dawn when the children's shows were just beginning, an envelope came through her letterbox with a loud clack. It was from Frank. 'Are you all right Marjorie?' the note said, and next to the words he had drawn a sunflower in charcoal with a proud and upright head.

A few hours later Marjorie wandered down the street with the specialist shops, a stream of sharply focused pictures springing at her, rapid, uneven. She felt grief closing in at the back of her throat as though she had swallowed sand. She looked down at the strange assortment of clothes that hung roughly from her shape. Everything was unclean and unflattering. Her regular habit of turning herself out well suddenly seemed like a sick lie. The little charade she played with herself that she was some kind of sultry temptress. A fool was what she was.

She saw the lined, parched faces of husbands and wives haggling bitterly over the smallest patches of land, the women heaving with deep, mutinous sorrow, and the men uncomprehending, horrified and at sea. She saw the grainy pores of angry faces, enlarged with venom. She heard a tangle of murderous asides. A man's perfectly ironed shirt crumpled as he clutched at his heart with his hand. She saw the most thoughtful and generous gestures swatted away without a second glance. She saw beautiful plates of food abandoned or smashed mid-quarrel. She felt the tallest and costliest of buildings teeming with elaborate pet-hates, swarms of insults blackening the air. She smelt the disappointment that clung to the slender man who longed for a second child and whose wife told him, 'Over my dead body.' She flinched as a crystal table-lamp was hurled at a woman's head. A couple before her who could have been the Braintrees were staring ruin in the face and ruin stared straight back, heartless, provocative.

Then another current came and a consuming fondness for her own parents welled up in her. She would have torn herself to pieces for them. The way her father picked up and handled a thing, a bit of cutlery or some curled and waxy orange peelings. The way her mother's taut, narrow form occasionally loosened itself into a setting, expanding unexpectedly into the new surroundings, into the new situation, like the lightest kind of exhalation.

Wearily, she continued for a mile or so, bland and uninvolved. She took a seat in a bakery that had a small café section in the back with cherry-red plastic chairs, which were stuck to the ground. She picked up an early edition of the evening paper that had been left there, jam-stained, grease-spotted. Another

American writer had taken up this slavery-reparation question. Marjorie tried to think straight. Was money the only way to express regret now? Were there not other sorts of making good that were subtler, harder, more sincere? To find the best way, didn't you have to sit down with the people who were hurting most and give them exactly what they desired?

Over her shoulder she heard some large women admiring the display in the bakery window. 'Oh, I could never have fruit cake after September. Don't even roast a chicken, although I might do a chicken dish, you know, a recipe. Otherwise it spoils Christmas, doesn't it?'

She flicked back to the beginning of the paper. Suddenly, from her mouth, there emerged a long, low howl. She put her hands to her eyes and shut them tight. Gingerly she opened them one at a time. The headline in front of her read 'DRUNKEN BUS SHAME OF TV NURSE SENSIBLE'. And there she was. Sprawled out unconscious on the upholstered bus seat, her mouth gaping and thick dribble, or worse, dripping down her chin.

Fears for TV's Nurse Dempsey were aroused last night when she was found unconscious on a night bus very much the worse for wear by one of our readers, amateur photographer Jake Myers. The makers of Nightingale Park *have so far declined to comment but a spokesperson for the National Union of Nurses issued a statement saying Nurse Dempsey had done the profession a huge disservice by her behaviour. Alcohol Alert UK says the levels of alcohol consumed by young women is on the increase and the amount required to render a person unconscious in this way would pose severe health risks to the individual. The Nurses'*

Union is engaged in pay talks with the government this week. It is possible that the four per cent rise they have negotiated may have been jeopardised by the behaviour of Nurse Dempsey, played by actress Eve Rice. Call 0848 637892 if you think Nurse Dempsey should be sacked by the TV station for setting a bad example to young women nationwide.

Nine

A few days passed. Marjorie lay in bed holding on to herself tightly. She thought of thinking, but there was a huge failure in language because it could get nowhere near the feelings themselves. Were there actual feelings? Marjorie did not know. Had anything happened or changed? Wasn't that how outcome usually worked? She peered through the window at the late-afternoon sky, its colours thin, indifferent, ailing, mechanical, inhuman. There was a sharp ring at the door but she just rolled over on to her side. It was less comfortable there. The shrill bell sounded again. The world looked all the same from this new angle. Marjorie measured it against the second hand of the clock. At forty-two seconds, the noise stopped. It couldn't be the press, could it? Hunting her down? The noise began again, and a minute and a half later it was still going. She would have to do something. She went downstairs and flung one of Hugh's coats round her shoulders when, really, it had not been her intention to start the day at all.

'Hello?' she muttered, through the letterbox.

'Mum, it's me.'

'Oh!'

'Can I come in?'

'I—'

May slipped into the front room, all sympathy and concern. 'Frank said to come,' she mentioned, but she asked no questions. Very gently, after seeking permission, she began silent tidying. The room looked like a deserted night street, littered with polystyrene and cardboard containers, dried-up pizza corners, biscuit boxes, chicken bones, snarl-edged half-sandwiches laced with mould. There were coats and scattered shoes on the floor and an ironing-board and a half-emptied sewing-box trailing tangled cotton reels and skeins of wool and an opened-out black paper envelope with neat silver rows of needles and pins.

May made omelettes with tomato, and toast, and they ate the meal together, both clearing their plates, and it was no longer possible not to say things. Marjorie looked around the room distractedly. 'How's your friend? You know, the one I saw that time. The man?'

May shook her head sadly. Tears sprang to Marjorie's eyes.

'No, it's all right. It's OK,' May said. 'It's for the best.'

'Really?'

May nodded. 'Frank came to see me. At the flat. He told me you weren't doing so great. So I thought I'd just—'

'No. Well.'

'He's a funny man, isn't he? I mean, nice and everything, but he's so ladylike.'

'Is he? Perhaps that's it.'

'He's ever so fond of you.'

'Yes. You're right. He is . . .'

'I thought maybe I could stay the night, in case you fancy a bit of company. If you'd like me to.'

'Thanks. I would like that.'

'Did I tell you they've just increased our rent? Again.'

'That must be——' Marjorie stopped speaking. 'Has it turned very, very cold?' she asked. She was shaking.

'Let's put you to bed, shall we? We can talk about everything tomorrow. Would you like a pot of Sleeptight?'

Marjorie was in the bathroom, putting on fresh night-things. In the bathroom mirror she watched May clear a little space and set down her insomniac's tea. On the night table a lone book was propped open. May turned it over and read a sentence out loud. '"The repetitive aspect of sequences of partnership is remarkably literal."' She read it again. She took a breath, thinking, thinking. 'You know, Mum, sometimes I think you should read more proper books, you know.'

'What's that, darling?'

'I was just saying, you know, maybe you should read more proper books, books about real people, reread your favourite novels again, maybe, rather than all this work stuff.'

Marjorie came into the bedroom and kissed her daughter softly on the head.

In the morning May went out early to the shops and came back with a compôte of dried fruit, which she served with natural yoghurt and honey to her mother in bed.

'May! May! Guess what.' Marjorie was elated. 'I slept

through the night,' she exclaimed. 'First time since you were born! Eight till eight, I can't believe it.'

'Thought I didn't hear anything.'

'What d'you mean, "didn't hear anything"?'

'Well, you do like a wander at night, don't you? I mean—'

'Don't say it used to disturb you.'

'Oh, no. Well, not really. Maybe a tiny bit.'

'And you never said anything. That's terrible – I had no idea.'

'It's nothing, honestly. It was reassuring in a funny way.'

'I don't know the first thing about being a mother, do I?'

'It doesn't matter at all, really.'

Marjorie sat up in bed, surrounded by blue-and-white striped pillows and half-drunk cups of lime-flower tea. 'Fetch me a pen and paper, would you, darling? I've so many letters to write.'

'Shouldn't you be resting?'

'I'm not ill or anything.'

'Mind if I do a bit more tidying? I'm in the mood now.'

'Lovely, darling. You are kind.' May wore an apron of red gingham and held a broom and a black rubbish sack.

Dear Eve (may I?)

This is a bizarre letter to have to write, but I feel the need to apologise for something that occurred last week which must have inconvenienced you terribly.

She put the letter to one side and began another.

Dear May

When you were about four months I found myself at a very low ebb. The loss of your father seemed very overwhelming, and although you were a huge comfort to me, the loveliest and most wonderful baby anyone could possibly imagine, I did find it hard to cope. Without really knowing what I was doing one day, I went out in the morning and left you on your own until the evening in your cot. This would have been a very shocking thing for a baby to have to experience. It is something I regret hugely and unreservedly. Nothing like that ever happened again, and very soon after I began to get my life together, in a funny way with your help because my huge feelings of love for you allowed me to . . . I want to apologise for this now because I feel it's important that I, that you

Marjorie fell asleep and woke in the early evening. The doorbell was ringing again, and it was her friend Bette. May showed her into the bedroom and left them to it, having taken their beverage orders.

Bette had been to a wedding and had come away a little mournful. 'I knew something was up when instead of thinking how beautiful the bride looked I kept noticing how shockingly the dressmaker had done the hem.'

'Was it that bad?'

'It was a disgrace, uneven, lumpy, and it looked like it would come down any minute. I know I'm probably just sick with jealousy but – and then they had to go and read that sonnet – you know, the one we hate.' She fished the order of service booklet out of her bag and passed it to Marjorie.

'"Let me not to the marriage of true minds admit impediments,"' Marjorie read. 'That has to be about my least favourite poem. How could anyone possibly think it was about true love?'

'I really don't know.'

'Sometimes I think the whole world spends so much time thinking about what love isn't, what it shouldn't do, what it can't run to.' Marjorie flicked through the pamphlet. 'Oh, they had that St Paul thing as well.'

'Yes, but I've never really got on with him.'

'I know. Exactly. I'm as much for faith, hope and charity as the next person, but why does he have to dwell on what love mustn't be? "Love does not behave itself unseemly, seeketh not her own, is not easily provoked, thinketh no evil, envieth not, vaunteth not itself,"' she read. 'You just can't legislate like that. I mean everyone has their off-days, don't they?'

'Too right,' agreed Bette. 'Their off-years, even.'

'Sometimes I think people fight so hard to make love all mysterious and elusive. Why don't they just say that if you can build a life with a person you're crazy about it's the biggest blessing in the world?'

Bette sighed and nodded. 'I suppose it's just that it doesn't always work out, though, does it? In the end, I mean.'

But Marjorie was gazing towards the window. 'I've always fancied that thing in Shakespeare when the daughter says she wouldn't have let her enemy's dog spend a night outside in a storm like that, not even if it had bitten her. I think that's what I'd call the real thing.'

Bette was nodding thoughtfully again. 'Although I've never been big on dogs, as you know.'

'Well, no, but you get the picture.' Bette was perched on the edge of Marjorie's bed, her hair falling in loose waves down her back. She scratched her head.

Just then May knocked lightly at the door and said, with a giggle, 'Someone else to see you, Mum.' She showed Frank into the room. 'Tea? Coffee, anyone? Cake? Something stronger?'

'Oh, yes, please.' Marjorie smiled. 'Can we have a selection?' Frank was hovering uncertainly by the bedside. She gestured towards a chair in the corner of the room, 'Bring it over,' she told him. He picked it up with the utmost care.

While his back was turned Bette, pink, grinning and astonished, mouthed to her friend, 'Where you been hiding him?'

May returned with a sort of impromptu picnic, a checked blanket, a large tray with teapots and cakes and sandwiches and a half-bottle of gin, which was all Marjorie had in in the way of drink. There was even a tumbler with four or five white freesias in it. Marjorie looked at her daughter with misty eyes. 'Everything you do, you do so beautifully,' she did not say. She did not wish to embarrass her in public.

Frank began a long story about painting in the Lake District, but Marjorie wasn't listening: she was watching her lodger through Bette's eyes. It seemed she regarded him as something of a god. She was enquiring acutely into his working methods, the sorts of paints he favoured, the kinds of hair his preferred brushes were fashioned from, did he stretch his own canvases? May gave Marjorie a wink, but Marjorie felt unsure. 'Oh, really? Rabbit glue? How extraordinary!' Bette drank in Frank's words as though they were huge cloudy symbols of high romance.

'Oh, for goodness' sake. Really!' Marjorie whispered, under her breath.

After Bette left and Frank left, Marjorie slept and dreamed wild dreams. She dreamed she was a dog snapping at the heels of the people she most loved.

Later on May came in, crunching an apple. 'Feeling much better,' Marjorie said. 'There's nothing wrong with me apart from stayinbeditis. I thought we might have a clear-out. What d'you think? Can you face it?'

'Sure.' May was smiling. 'Shall we start with the bed-room?'

'We could do,' Marjorie said. 'In fact, I've got something to show you.'

She hopped out of bed, knelt on the floor and dragged the seventeen-year-old Christmas stocking from under the pleated valance.

'I thought we might open this together. It's from your father. He was so organised with things like that. He did it before he died.'

'And you've been keeping it all this time?'

'Not like that. It was lost and I came across it a few weeks ago, and then I suppose I thought it was something we could do together, maybe. I was saving it for a rainy day. I opened a couple of things without you. I hope you don't mind. At first I thought it was from me to him. But now I remember him mentioning it. "It's all done," he said. He went out one Saturday and came back saying he'd taken care of it all. I can't believe I could have forgotten. Here, sit down.' May took a rapid step back. 'We don't have to if you don't want to . . .'

'No, it's just . . . it's just a bit . . .'

Marjorie placed the woollen limb in May's arms and May

regarded it gravely. 'And I would have been four and a half months old.'

'That's right.'

'Can a four-and-a-half-month-old baby unwrap presents?'

'Well, no, not really.'

'Why did he do it for me, then?'

'What's that?'

'Why would he go to the trouble of making me a whole Christmas stocking when I was too young to know what it was?'

'For you? Oh, I see. Well, it's obvious, isn't it? Because he adored you, of course.'

'D'you think?'

'I'm a hundred per cent certain. And I'm guessing . . .' Marjorie spoke slowly but thought fast, '. . . I'm guessing that because you were so young and everything, a lot of the things in the stocking would be for, you know, an older type of child or . . . or person. I mean, there's not a huge amount of choice for people of that age, is there? A lot of things are a choking hazard and so on. Also, in a baby's first year it's quite usual to be given things for when you're grown-up, you know, fountain pens and silver knick-knacks and so on. Er . . . toiletries.'

'See what you mean,' May said solemnly.

'Of course, we don't have to open it now. We could easily do it another time, when we're both a bit more on top of things. When we're both a bit more ourself.'

'I suppose I could take it home with me, couldn't I? Did I say the landlord's almost doubled the rent?' May had the stocking cradled in her arms.

Marjorie's mind spun with all sorts of rapid calculations.

If she could just create some kind of diversion, wrest the stocking from her and substitute the old parcels meant for Marjorie for new ones suitable for a baby girl. She could use the same paper, rough up the presents a bit so they'd seem seventeen years old. Her head was racing. It was hardly international subterfuge. There was always old stock and market stalls and—

'Why don't we keep it for another day?' Marjorie suggested lightly. She could get out to the shops this afternoon, even.

May drew all the parcels out of the stocking. There were eleven in all and she handled them nervously, with extreme caution, as though they were little infants of her own. 'This is so weird.'

'We don't have to do it now.'

May nodded sadly. Her hands were shaking. Extremely slowly, she began unwrapping a parcel, making sure not to tear any of the holly-strewn paper. The holly was now a thin light blue colour. It looked Victorian. Some of the paper fell into brittle strips in May's hands. It was warm and dry under the bed and lighter than you would expect. The packet contained two pairs of woollen doll's tights, one pair pink with fluffy yellow chicks running up and down the leg. The other was unpatterned pale pistachio with two bobbly seams at the top.

Marjorie's entire body slumped with relief into her chair.

'Mum, you must have bought these.'

'No. It was all Dad.'

'You mean he went into a toy shop and chose them himself?'

'I know. It's amazing.'

'He did all that just for me?'

'Of course. He thought the world of you. He adored you. The day you were born was the best day of his life.' It was true.

May was smiling softly, but her cheeks were glossy with tears. 'Sometimes I feel like the world is just too dangerous, you know.'

Marjorie nodded. 'It is very dangerous,' she said softly.

'But there's nowhere else, is there? Is there?'

'Not really. I mean I suppose there's other people's worlds but in the end—'

'But they're even worse, aren't they?'

'They can be. They can be.'

'Yeah. Sometimes I'm terrified that when I look back I won't even have any memories.'

'Oh, darling.'

'What I don't understand is how can someone adore you one minute and totally abandon you the next? But I see it everywhere. Why won't people just have their feelings permanently? I don't mean for ever but at least, you know – I mean . . . What do the books say?' May gestured towards the shelves that lined the room.

'Well, I don't know about books but I suppose the main trap people fall into is turning the battles that go on inside each person individually into a kind of war that is going on between the two of them.'

'That's terrible.'

'It can be, but if you can get through all that nonsense and build a life together with someone you're mad about it's the biggest blessing of your life.'

May smiled shyly. 'Did you have to, like, go through all that kind of stuff with Dad, then? Getting all muddled up and sorting it out and everything?'

'No, no, I didn't. Not really.'

'Because everything was all right anyway?'

'Well, more because there was no time.' Marjorie looked away. 'There wasn't really any time at all. It was over so quickly somehow. We knew each other for less than three years and then . . . before I even had the chance to—'

May looked up suddenly. Marjorie lowered her head. 'I suppose when I look back at my life, it's you that I've really been craziest about,' she did not say. And then something amazing happened. She did say it.

May turned immediately the colour of a radish. Marjorie was overcome with shame. She hung her head low. You could not just shovel your emotions on to another person like that when you had no idea what kind of mood they were in or whether they . . . or what they even – but when her daughter looked up she was smiling broadly. 'Oh, Mum!' she said. And then, good-humouredly planting a kiss squarely on her mother's flushed cheek, 'Look, isn't it about time you found someone your own age to pick on?'

May's fingers began unwrapping the nearest parcel, which was a red plastic baby's cutlery set with her name embossed on the handles in gold lettering. She looked smooth and happy.

'Those I have seen before,' Marjorie said. 'He sent off for them from a mail-order catalogue shortly after you were born.' May inserted the box back into its wrappings and retied its pink ribbon.

'I think I'm going to keep the rest until Christmas,' May announced. 'If that's all right with everybody else.'

'Sure,' Marjorie said. 'Why not?'

The following day Marjorie rose at lunchtime and dressed in her navy skirt and her best red-and-white chevron-patterned bell-sleeved chiffon blouse. Between the kite shop and the Swedish food store, a small boutique she hadn't noticed before was being refurbished. Some men in dusty over-alls were laying a dark-wood floor. Marjorie peered round the door. 'D'you know what this shop's going to be?' she enquired.

'Hasn't been let yet,' the nearer man said, without looking up.

'Oh, right.'

'D'you know what the rent is? Is there much space through the back? Is the flat upstairs empty, d'you know? Can I have a little poke round?'

Both men looked up. 'How many you had?' the further-away man asked.

'Sorry?'

'How many drinks you had?' The men cackled hoarsely.

'Funny,' Marjorie said. 'Funny.'

She went into the Gammon Rasher, which was brightly lit and steamy, and ordered a cup of black tea and a slice of something sweet, 'You choose,' she said to the waiter, who smelt strongly of deodorant. His lower face and neck were livid with acne.

A woman was talking to him about her day. One of her dancing shoes had been stolen from her bag on the bus. It was beautiful, she'd never find its like again. 'What use is one shoe to anybody?' she asked. 'What use is one shoe?' She was on a run of bad luck, she explained. The week before, twenty pounds had vanished from her purse, just like that, and when she'd reached for it at the supermarket it had disappeared into thin air; she'd had to put all her shopping back. She must have dropped it. Then, the week before that, her mother had died.

Marjorie sat at a round table and began to write her letter to May again. She put her pen down. You could spend a lifetime rehearsing apologies or seeking them, agonising over the wording. And who were you doing it for exactly? Wasn't the best thing just to keep on trying to improve things in the smallest ways? A sort of conscientiousness, was it? Isn't that what true optimism was? And bringing yourself freshly to every new situation undefended, without a mountain of plights and gripes towering behind you at all times?

Marjorie saw the waiter set three cups and saucers and three cakes in front of a trio of elderly ladies, who flirted with him mildly as if it were the most daring act in the world. 'If I was fifty years younger,' they said. The waiter, whose name was Joe, blushed deeply and scratched his painful-looking neck, and smiled as the women divided their cakes into three and passed the slices round between them so that they could all enjoy a taste of everything. Through the window she saw that Sew Be It was closing down. Removal men were dismantling some of the shop fittings and hurling them into a nearby skip. They looked tired, their faces streaked with sweat, and they slumped on the pavement and shared a tin of Coke. From nowhere she imagined the Braintrees' child, a blondish, long-limbed boy with an enormous forehead, who argued incessantly with an elderly nanny who idolised him.

The waiter brought her the tea and a slice of paradise cake, which was iced in white with a dark brown pattern of feathering. 'How're things?' she asked him. He nodded shyly, three or four times, his head low, eyes fixed to the ground. The little white heads on his spots looked so angry and sad.

'You?' he enquired gruffly, with an embarrassed smile.

'Oh, well, I suppose, in a lot of ways, everything's been a bit mad lately but the thing is I'm half thinking of opening a shop. I'm wondering about having a break from the counselling work I've been doing. Take a lease for a year at first. There's a nice little shop free a few streets from my house. It's not expensive. There's a little flat above, tiny, but it's got a balcony and this really sweet baby-sized blue kitchen. It might do for my daughter.'

'What would you sell?'

'I don't know yet. I've got to think about that. It's going to be the kind of shop that's more about the shopkeeper than – than the merchandise.'

Joe bit back a grin. 'Is that right?'

'There'll be something for everyone. Somewhere people can come to, just if they want or need to. Oh you know. They won't have to buy anything if they don't want, and everything will be dirt cheap anyway so it won't make much difference – obviously I'm making this up as I go along – but there'll be tons of comfy chairs everywhere to sit on and we'll just provide the things that people really need in order to, you know, keep going . . . I don't know. To survive. There'll be cups of tea and everything and cake, and nothing will cost much, but it will be a proper shop. We'll have the newspapers and nice music and friendly staff with loads of experience who love a chat. I know I'm talking nonsense but you do know what I mean, don't you?'

There was a small pause. 'My nan's got a newsagent and it's really hard work,' he offered, finally.

Marjorie pressed a ball of cake against her saucer with the back of her spoon. Perhaps she needed a few more days off work to think about everything. She could ring in and say she was still indisposed – see that her clients were alerted in good time. The Braintrees might not even notice she was gone. She imagined them chatting away happily to an empty chair, their discordant, spry knockabout filling the air. It might be just what the doctor ordered. Through the window of the café she saw Frank dragging his laundry behind him in huge, square, red-checked bags. 'Life goes on,' she said. Could you love him maybe? Don't be absurd! She giggled.

Later she would telephone May to see if she could be persuaded to a matinée tomorrow, or she could try Bette at the bank. Take herself off on an outing, that's what she would do. She could ask Frank. Once a month, more or less, she and Hugh had had a day trip to the seaside with sandwiches and a portable radio, rain or shine. Hugh said you should let external things, like money and the weather, influence the way you led your life as little as possible. She closed her eyes for a second. If he walked in through the door right now she would take him back like a shot. He would get her out of the mess she was in. He always knew the right thing to do. He was very adult in that way. (So many people specialised in knowing what you shouldn't do, which was often no help at all and essentially childish.) She was thinking hard now, straining, but the thing is, she would say, 'I just might not quite be able to carry on any more. In the same way. You know?' He would understand, but his understanding would be a light thing: it would not flatten her. It wouldn't take away the good things she did have. She imagined the two of them sitting on chairs in a room with an electric fire glowing in the grate. 'I just love you so much,' she said smoothly. 'So much.'

There was a train timetable in her handbag and she stopped to search for it. The bag had been elegant once but had suffered severely from overstuffing. She would buy a new one. Why not? She thought of the perfect away-day attire: apple-green knee-length tweed skirt with inverted pleat, pale grey jersey with a collar and three mother-of-pearl buttons. But she did not own these garments, never had. A pair of gold earrings – but what if, when she went to lift them from their padded velour lair, she did not quite have the heart? Not to worry, she said. It doesn't matter. You can always try again later, she said.

Your handbag represents your world in miniature, she thought, as she sifted through the assorted scraps of paper and dry crumbs. She liked to save anything impressive so that if she was ever caught out in some way, drowning or in a car smash, they would piece together good things about her. She would like people to know she thought nothing of buying a hot drink in a café most days. She was not mean with herself. The train timetable, when she finally found it, was two years out of date, but the very next moment Marjorie was fingering a crumpled receipt that had her writing on it – the advertisement from the baker's window she had scribbled down. 'Part-time housekeeper sought for two weeks (wife gone away) luxury apartment live-in.'

All the housekeepers she could remember in films were so thin! A housekeeper was a bit like a nurse, she thought, as she paid and made her way to the café door. A nurse crossed with a wife.

A few minutes later she was squeezing herself into the telephone kiosk at the end of her street and dialling the number. How dare she? But she did dare, and in the back of her head, where her nerves jangled terribly, there was even a mild sense of triumph.

'Colman?'

'Er, yes, hello. It's, er . . . My name's Marjorie. I'm calling about the housekeeping job.'

'That's good news. May I ask your age, Marjorie?'

'I'm forty-two.'

'When could you come, do you think? I'm at St John's Wood.'

'I could come now if you like.'

The man at the door was sincere-looking, his light eyes watery and alert. Although tall, his build was narrow, but the narrowness was surprising, like some kind of new development, because in all other ways he seemed so substantial. Dressed in loose grey trousers and a thin white shirt, which was exceptionally well ironed, he smelt faintly of limes. His name was Harold Colman, he said. He smiled. Marjorie stepped into the drawing room, with its dark walls and heavy red chenille curtains, its pair of plump sofas, the circular table loaded with thick books and a box of Romeo y Julietas, and beside that a pair of bow-backed satinwood chairs. He offered her a seat and asked if she would like some coffee. It was very grown-up.

Marjorie nodded and he disappeared, then returned with a silver tray that rattled in his hands. On a mantelpiece were many framed pictures of children who looked hundreds of years old, pale, unreachable, ghostly. In their stiff white clothes they rode in carriages pulled by glossy horses, or stood in small, formal groups on a lawn, gathered under the sure branches of an ancient tree.

'My family,' he said dreamily. 'That's my father and his four brothers. And now I'm practically the only one left!' Very carefully, he poured out the coffee into pink-and-gold rose-patterned cups and offered her cream and a Danish pastry and a tea plate and a linen napkin.

'When is your wife actually going away?' Marjorie enquired, balancing everything on her knee, licking a slick of icing from the corner of her mouth.

'She's gone already. In actual fact.'

'And you haven't found anyone yet?'

He shook his head. 'No one suitable, no.'

'Can I ask a little about the job? I imagine you'd like me to prepare your meals and—'

'Oh, do you cook? I mean, do you like cooking?'

'Oh, yes. I find it really soothing.'

'Do you? That's good. And what sort of dishes do you make?'

'I'd make whatever you like, of course.' She sounded

businesslike, professional. 'All your favourites,' she added, smiling. Where was the harm? 'I can follow a recipe.'

'That's very good,' the man said approvingly. 'Thank you very much.'

'That's all right. And what would my other, er . . . I mean, what else would you want me to do?'

'A little shopping possibly. The butcher and the fishmonger and the greengrocer all deliver. I suppose taking care of the house, although Hannah comes in to clean and iron. I'm meant to walk a lot. I don't know if that would interest you. You'd have a lot of time to yourself. You'd be the boss!' He smiled. 'I'm not what anyone could call difficult.'

'No, of course, I didn't think for a moment . . .' Marjorie coloured a little.

'And . . . the pay would be extremely—'

'Let's talk about that later.' She could not quite bear him to name a sum.

'As you like.'

Marjorie bit her lip. She had hurt his feelings with her clumsy delicacy. Why was it always, always, always the same? But when she glanced at him briefly, the man looked rather resilient. If anything, it occurred to her, he seemed faintly amused as he took the conversation on. 'Is there anything else you'd like to ask me?'

'I can't think.'

'Well, I've no doubts at all that you could do the job perfectly. Do you think it might suit you? Would you like me to show you the room? Or—'

'Goodness,' Marjorie said. 'I'm sure there's more things we need to talk about before—'

'That's all right. There's no rush.' They sat awkwardly together for some time under the childish eyes of the man's ancestors. In one picture the boys and girls looked carefree and partyish at a family picnic. A cloth was laid with pies and jellies and a whole salmon on a silver dish, and the smallest children's faces were flushed – from sugar, was it? From the sun? A dark girl, rounded in her sailorsuit, sat cross-legged a little outside the group, reading from a large book, her shoulders hunched, her eyes studious and slightly melancholy. Marjorie felt the red-and-white silk of her own shirt straining slightly at the chest. It was time to go. But the man's mouth was opening. 'Have you had lunch yet? Because I haven't.'

'Oh dear, did you want me to prepare something?'

'Well, I'm ashamed to say there's no food in the house, but perhaps we could go to the little place on the corner for a bite to eat. What do you think?'

Marjorie started coughing: a bit of sugar pastry was stuck in her throat and she quickly gulped some coffee, which dislodged the large crumb. With immense regret she peered at the three dark drips that now spotted her blouse.

'Oh, bad luck,' the man said, with feeling, and he darted into the kitchen, then returned with a moistened cloth.

Marjorie dabbed at herself shyly, but at least it gave her time to think. It couldn't actually hurt, could it? The lunch? Marjorie did not know. She smiled evenly, but there were things to clear up before they could think about . . . 'There is something I'd like to ask you.'

'Be my guest.'

'May I ask when your wife is planning to coming back?'

'Ah,' he said. 'It's all a bit up in the air.'

Marjorie stood up gently. 'She isn't coming back, is she?'

'No,' the man said. 'No, she's not. I'm sorry,' he added softly.

'No, I'm sorry.'

'Well, it's hardly your fault.'

'True.'

The man paced the room. 'She didn't leave me, it's nothing like that. We were extremely happy, but then she got ill and it went away for a bit so we let ourselves relax, but then it came back stronger than ever the following year, and almost before we realised what was going on it was too late. D'you see?'

Marjorie nodded. 'Yes,' she said.

'The odd thing is, I can't really seem to manage any more. Nothing seems to work. I mean, in me. I can't seem to – or, at any rate, I don't seem to want to do anything at all. You must think me a ridiculous idiot.'

'Not for a second,' Marjorie said.

'I just can't seem to—' He stopped talking and Marjorie thought he would cry.

After about a minute she asked, 'How long ago did she die?'

'Almost five years.'

'And had you been married a long time?'

'Forty-two years. And the maddest thing is, in some ways I never really knew her, I just sort of admired her from afar.' He drew a handkerchief out of his pocket and wiped his eyes. 'She was so beautiful-looking, and in her behaviour, I don't mean when she was ill, but even then.' His eyes, which had brightened considerably, closed and then he sighed. 'How is it you're so easy to talk to? I've never said any of this before.'

He looked up at Marjorie, who lowered her eyes sadly to her knees. 'And what about you?' he asked, after a little while.

'Oh!' she said. 'Me?'

'Yes.'

'Well, I'm really nothing much, um, really, I mean, there's not much to say . . .'

He laughed. 'Come with me to the corner and have a bite to eat. They know me in there. They'll look after us. It's not as hot as it is here. We can talk and you can tell me everything.'

Marjorie cast her eyes about the restaurant. It was almost three and only one other table of diners remained, an elderly couple, the woman, tall and handsome, making emphatic hand gestures, slicing the air with her palm, as the smaller man looked nervous and unhappy. You could feel him shrinking from her. It was agonising to observe. But suddenly, from nowhere, there were great hoots of laughter that went on and on, and everything about the woman's face was smiling. The man wound his watch bashfully and dropped a celebratory lump of sugar into his cup, then took up the woman's plump hand. You must have read it wrong somehow, Marjorie reprimanded herself, mistaken something that was merely grave for a species of hostility. Still, it was a relief.

She turned away. The place was grander than she had imagined, with white tablecloths and polished glass. The waiter recommended the sole.

'Will you tell me about yourself?' the man asked.

'Oh, no,' Marjorie said. 'I feel too silly.'

'Silly?'

'Oh, you know what it's like. I'm sure there's nothing that would really—'

'Let me be the judge of that.'

'What sort of thing are you thinking?'

'Anything. Everything.'

'D'you mean references and so on?'

'Oh, no! Nothing like that.'

'What, then?'

'I don't know. Tell me how you are. What you're thinking. What your plans are. Your hopes. What's been going on with you. I'd like to know. If you don't mind. I'd like to – well, I'd like to help, if I may.'

'Would you?' Marjorie's eyes widened, and just then the waiter brought over an oval platter, bearing a gold-flecked sole and a halved lemon upholstered in a square of white muslin. She picked up her fork and freed the pale flakes of fish from the central bone. 'Would you really?'

He nodded seriously. 'Start at the beginning.' He made to take her hand across the table, but just then Marjorie sprang to her feet. 'What's the matter?' he asked.

'Well, I just feel, what I feel is—' She smoothed down her skirt. Her gaze fell on the other couple in the restaurant, who were making their way out of the room: he such a delicate little creature and she so strong-looking, it would have been barely surprising had she bent to pick him up.

Marjorie thought of Homer Rise and of quite how much she liked it, and of May and Bette and Frank and their routine unfailing love. She smiled broadly. (Was Frank's infuriating evening clamour merely designed to place him in her thoughts late at night? Well, if that was so, it certainly worked.) She smiled again and bit her top lip.

Suddenly she made a huge tower in her mind of all that life could offer: the gains and steep losses, the pleasure and conflict and boredom and comforts and love. If she could just open things out a little . . . take some of the stacked furniture away from the doors. A snatch of a song about Paris that Hugh had liked came at her, comic and intense.

She closed her eyes briefly, thinking, thinking. Then she turned to face the man. 'The thing is,' she said softly – it was clear now, 'what I want to say is, thank you very much but – but, no, no, thank you. It's not for me. The job. And I'm not for, um, er, it. You see, the thing is I've got so much to be getting on with myself. I've already got my work cut out, in fact, and there's so much that needs doing, and I just didn't realise,' and with that she pressed herself through the restaurant's plate-glass doors and into the cool, thin rain that fell gently on to her face. Then she gave a little unexpected cry of joy.

Acknowledgements

With thanks to:

Wendy Perriam
Tom Aster
Kate MacKenzie Davey
Geraldine Cooke
Janice Brent
Caroline Dawnay
Sarah Ballard
Victoria Harrison